Short Works

by
Cameron H. Chambers

a compilation of the author's previously
unpublished shorter pieces

Also by Cameron H. Chambers:

Vignetta Vendetta Slices of Life

The Man Who Saved the Planet

English Composition One

Three Novellas

Don't Cross the Devil

Confessions of an Internet Don Juan

The Stone Cabin

For the Love of a Madman

Short Works
Acknowledgments

Logo by Jelena
The Runaway Dominatrix inspired by Christina
A Modest Proposal ending inspired by Kristina
The Adventures of Franchesska dedicated to the loving memory of Anthony

Dedicated to Libby, Bill, mom, Sue, Jelena, Rachael, Lonnie, Janis, Donald Shea, Anna Ruth Diaz, Angeline, Christina, Kristina, Seth, Alex, Anthony, Kimberly Fracassi, and The Gladiator...and so it goes...and on and on it goes...straight on till morning...third star on the left...

Twins
by
Cameron H. Chambers

The wind made a ghastly howl; its presence felt unnatural. It sounded like an act of torture upon a small animal, or in my inebriated, paranoid state, a baby screaming for its inattentive mother. I hear similar cries in my dreams often. There are two distinct voices, one a boy's, the other a girl's, and the voices never age or mature. They have remained those of children over the years. They are stuck somewhere, chiefly in my mind, but are perhaps from some intangible dimension. I hear the cries on playgrounds frequently, at malls, often whimpering for their mothers. It drives a chill right through my spine. I want to shout at these children, these disembodied voices, the voices of the small boys in particular, "Do it yourself, man. Tie your own goddamn shoe. Can't you see she's busy?" But the reality is they are never the voices of my own children. Nor would I dare speak to any child in that manner. My frustration and pain get the best of me. Since my twins passed away a few years ago, I am haunted every moment. There has rarely been a minute of sleep. I can't watch a program on television with children in it. The zoo, the park, the grocery store, so many places are unwelcome destinations to me now.

I went insane. I had no choice. Otherwise, I should have certainly perished. To have your children, a twin boy and girl—your own flesh—die a miserable cold, soggy death at your own hand, because you were drunk on your day off and ran your small car off the road into a flooded ditch, is an ignominious fate. And well it should be. Should I expect some reward? The car immediately filled with water. It had rained volumes that week. The twins were in the backseat. They both cried for their mother who was not in the car. At so tender an age, they understood that their daddy was useless. I have been a voracious smoker for so long now, over thirty years, I knew I could not hold my breath long enough to disengage myself from my seatbelt in the rapidly filling car, force the window down, and get my twins out. They drowned in three feet of water. I am haunted by their faces. I can no longer speak their names. I can barely turn on the faucet or the garden hose now. The sight of running water strikes terror throughout my crippled, diseased mind. I took as deep of a breath as

I could with my clogged, raspy lungs and went back under to get my charges, but it was too late. I know now the torment of the insane for my recompense. And tonight bespeaks another hideous lesson.

My newly-found friends and I had gathered at my house. It is a sturdy structure, double-coursed brick with iron rebar up the length of the walls and dripped concrete throughout the inside frame. I can hardly drill a wall in my home; it is so solid. If any house was built to withstand a hurricane, it would be mine. Conflict, tragedy, the horrors of life not only find me, they seek me out. I was most uneasy about tonight's circumstance. Julie and her clapboard house, with the insect-ridden T-111 extending down the sides of her home into the dirt, and the beams in her ceiling twenty-four inches apart (mine are twelve), would likely not have a home to return to after tonight. It was now the eye of the storm, but the worst winds were coming. Amazingly, we still had electricity from the generator, but it was almost out of gas. I could feel the tremendous gusts of the second half of the carnival show barreling down on us. The lightning danced through every room. It would fly through a window and out the one across from it, zigging and zagging precariously. Then the thunder clapped like a mighty titan. It would not be much longer before the lights would go out. We all remained in a sedate, but somewhat jovial mood, the influence of the alcohol perhaps, but underneath our thin veneer, everyone was terrified. My skin was crawling from the inside out, but as the older and wiser of my company, I had to remain the more stoic.

"They said eighteen inches have fallen on the Westside," Julie called in from my family room. She seemed fearless, watching in my family room the lone station on television brave enough to continue broadcasting. The rectangular room has eighteen windows from which to observe the cruelty of nature. Julie drew a certain energy from the storm. Her boyfriend James and I, and my friend, Sara, sat at my dining room table in the next room. There were no windows and the outside walls were at least a foot thick.

"Well, we're flooded out for sure," James called into her. They were originally from mountain country in Colorado, not Florida, which is where we all found ourselves residing for one reason or another, and they understood flooding, but not this eerie, creeping, insidious wind and rainstorm. "Our street is under water by now," James said turning to Sara and me. He hoisted his beer and swallowed in his reluctant, pensive awareness.

My house came ready-made with a moat. The sight of a ditch in the front yard of the house I thought to buy seemed the nastiest of ironies. I had first seen my home over the Internet, and I did not know there was a partly exposed culvert running most of the property. God can be so exacting. I thought I had done my penance, but I guess penance is never enough. I had to move here quickly to seize the job I wanted, so I bought the house. It was one in a series of hasty decisions. I had felt until now that the drainage ditch in the front yard was unsightly and a mosquito hatchery, but after the comparable rains on this side of town, we were still high above it all and relatively dry.

Debris rumbled and collided around the neighborhood and was scattered all over the street, up and down it, from large branches of magnolias and pines, and pine cones of various assortments, to garbage can lids left atop their cans by unthinking or inexperienced neighbors, who had no sort of idea what these winds can do. The rain is life-threatening, the lightning intense and frightening, but the wind is the true danger. A pebble, if launched properly, can yield a devastating blow. I have seen a single pine needle, a flimsy, delicate object, piercing through the diameter of a telephone pole as if an arrow shot from a bow. The odd potted plant rustled around and tipped whimsically this way and that, or had been shattered earlier on; a few went rolling down the water-filled channels, cascading along as they spun in oblongs down the drenched street. I could witness all this from the many windows of my home. I was reminded of a newspaper photograph of a young man riding his bicycle through waist-high waters. The photo had made me laugh. It was four in the afternoon and the streetlamps had been on all day. The winds now were probably only thirty miles per hour in the eye of the storm. The local news station had registered sustained winds at ninety and gusting to one hundred and twenty just over an hour ago. We waited with the anxiety of knowing that to wait was all we could do. Sara, who had been sitting quietly, asked, "are we going to be all right? I've heard the second half of one of these storms is the worst." Sara is a young gal, straight out of graduate school from Michigan State, and this was her fricane. She was outwardly nervous, and I wanted to comfort her.

"This house is rugged. I swear by it." I prayed mentally as I said that. I have tempted fate too many times and I have felt its angry lash against my back.

"Should we go to a shelter?" Sara asked.

"It's too late. There are too many downed power lines and downed trees between here and there...we couldn't make it, if we wanted to. It is best to ride this out here." Just then there was huge crack louder than any shotgun or overloaded transformer as a tremendous gust caught an unsuspecting tree and ripped through its limbs. Julie scurried in from the family room.

"Did you see it?" James asked.

"No, and I don't want to. It was in the backyard," Julie said. Her tune of autonomy had changed. My neighbor has a huge oak that tips over his house, dripping soft, cool shade on the warm evenings. I wondered if there would be more of us arriving soon. The last hurricane I was in, I was a child not much older than my little ones I remembered, and an oak, rotted at its base, had fallen right through the center of my parents' house. It effectively separated and cut off my brothers and sisters and me from our parents, who were just down the hall. We could talk to one another over the rumble of thunder and the rain slashing at our tiny faces, over the huge trunk that stood at its width taller than my height, but, we, the children had to ride out the storm on our own. I remember my father calling words of encouragement to us, his voice eerily lofting in as if from some distant plane, and his barking instructions at my older brother.

The familiar deafening screams of the small children played over again in my head. I heard the twins crying out first for their mother and then their drunken father. I had to keep it together. I was the only one among us who had gone through a hurricane before. James and Julie had lived in Florida some time, but they too, as Sara, are younger and had never lived until now to witness a hurricane in all its unsheathed magic and glory and the complete destruction it leaves in its wake.

Then the lights flickered and went out. Sara noisily cried out from somewhere deep in her throat, a guttural and startled warning of a snared animal.

"It's okay," I said. Me, the stoic, I thought. I nearly laughed aloud at the thought. "We have flashlights and candles," I said as I busied myself striking a match. My hands trembled, but no one could see in the darkness. I lit the candelabra I had placed on the table. Sara looked so angelic by the soft light. "There. That's not so bad," I said cooing. I reminded myself of patching up bruised elbows and knees when I had been a father and husband. Of course, my wife had left me. I had effectively ended her life as well.

I heard a voice shoot through me. "Daddy," it cried. I looked in a panic, but there was no one and nothing there.

"What's wrong?" Sara asked.

"Nothing." I decided I needed something stronger and poured a whiskey. Beer would no longer fit the bill.

"How are we going to pee?" Sara asked.

"The plumbing still works, right?" James inquired.

"Yeah. Plumbing is not electric," I informed Sara. "You can flush. When the tank runs empty, dump in a bucket of water. Gravity will flush the bowl. I filled up the bathtub. There's a bucket next to it."

"I never knew that," Sara said.
"They didn't teach you that in grad school?" Julie said. It was meant to be funny, but Sara took it as a snippy remark. Julie had not finished college. Her comments about school were suspect. The tension was showing on everyone's face, even by the agreeable luster of the candles. "I have a battery-operated cd player. Something mellow, Sara?" I asked.

"Hey There Delilah." "I love that song." She had seen the compact disk at my house previously. The song sadly lilted in and I breathed out a little tension. Seconds later, a very unnatural sound drowned out the melodic din in the room; it was one of breaking glass. It had the ferocity of a car bomb and again we were bathed in darkness. I froze. I thought I had imagined the noise at first, dreamily reaching inside my mind for something to hold onto, but this time it was valiant Julie crying out in her murky anguish, snapping me to attention. A branch had flown through a family room window, spraying glass as far as the tiled kitchen floor. The wind kicked around the blinds, holding them upright in a horizontal position as though some deceit of levitation and the noise of the air rushing in hissed menacingly at me.

"Do something! Do something!" It was Sara screaming. Again, I didn't realize at first it was a human voice. The wind cried and I could hear the wood floors of my home squeak in pain.

"We'll be okay," I shouted. "Put your shoes back on. There's glass," I said more calmly. "And stay in here." I followed my next instinct and brought the cooler with the ice and drinks from the kitchen into the dining room. I could feel the blast of wet air in my face as I entered the kitchen. "The eye has moved on," I said. I expected my guests might not understand my cryptic remark, but I did not wish to frighten them more. I knew we were in for rough waters.

Suddenly, there was a succession of breaking glass. "I can't take this," Sara cried. "Take me to a shelter before it's too late. Get me out of here."

"It is too late," I said. I heard glass ornaments and objects fly off of shelves and crash thunderously in other rooms. The more the wind kicked up, the more the deafening cries of my twins grew. "Shut up," I yelled. I immediately and awkwardly explained to Sara that I did not mean for her to shut up. She then insisted we go to a shelter and got up from her chair in preparation to face the storm outside. She would not remain trapped in a house, rapidly deteriorating, with some sort of madman. Julie chimed in as well. "I agree. Let's go now. James, get my keys."

"We're blocked in," he answered.

"I'll drive," I said. Not a one of them knew where the nearest shelter even was, and though I felt this was folly, I knew I had to lead them to safety. Just then a mighty crack from the lightning produced an eerie ripping sound that soon followed; it was as discordant as tearing a stack of junk mail into pieces making the useless items ready for the garbage. The shingles started popping off the roof one by one. I knew what would happen next. The entire roof might lift off. We would, in fact, have to leave my home for the security of the city shelter, a public high school about three miles away. I prayed silently and more intently.

Julie and James piled as quickly as possible into the backseat of my compact car. Sara sat up front with me. In the few seconds it took us to leave by the front door, struggling to open it against the negative pressure of the winds, and climb in the car, we were completely soaked. The tops of the trees in my yard were bending, almost kissing the street below them and the wind lashed everything around in anger. We were pulling out of my short driveway, and a masterful bolt of lightning lit up the sky for the flash of a half second, and I heard in my ear, right next to me, Sara scream, "look out."

A massive pine tree, a victim of the lightning, fell across the driveway and onto the car, so I steered abruptly to counter the potential deadly effects of the tree's falling, which surely was going to crush us all, and I unintentionally ran off the driveway and into the ditch.

It was two days later. I had lain mostly unconscious on the embankment of my front lawn until a city crew, which had started cleaning up my neighborhood, discovered me. I was wheeled on a gurney by EMTs to a local emergency room. Triage was setup in the parking lot of the overrun hospital. A nurse attended to the lacerations on my head and face, as I drifted in and out of consciousness.

"What's the story with this one?" I could hear the man's voice who asked the question. He sounded like he was in charge and probably a doctor.

"A clean-up crew found him almost underwater in a ditch. A tree had fallen on his car. There were two females and a male trapped in the car, crushed. I think he will be okay. Minor broken bones. A concussion.

He remembers his name and address, so there doesn't seem to be any memory loss. He was face down in the mud they told me. I wonder how he made it," the nurse said.

"I guess he's lucky," the doctor said.

#######

A Modest Proposal for Future Generations
A Concise Argument in Favor of Age Enhancement in the U.S.
by
Cameron H. Chambers

I can almost totally eliminate the costs and payments of Medicare and drastically reduce or possibly eradicate altogether ongoing and future payments for anyone that might receive Social Security. I can curtail much of the cost of some expensive medical equipment and research, Alzheimer's as a notable choice. I can politely suggest a plan to extinguish the surplus population, who drain our resources, economic and otherwise, on a daily basis. If my plan is enacted, it could possibly balance the federal budget and give our remaining citizens a much needed bonus in a few scant years. So, what is it, you ask. Mandatory euthanasia for everyone at the age of 60 years. Think of the benefits for a moment. Please try not to be immediately repulsed by the idea. It has merit I assure you. I implore you to read on.

There are far too many people in this world already. America has easily jumped past the 300 million mark. The world's population is in the seven billion range, slightly higher, and growing exponentially. The earth, which cannot handle its enormous and explosive numbers already, will have an estimated 20 billion inhabitants in the next 20 to 30 years. And far too many of them are too aged and in the dusk of uselessness as to be considered active and productive members of our society. We need to start a grand plan in our own backyard. What if the American government were to put in place a sympathetic, systematic, benign, wide sweeping, and cost saving program to enhance the average age of our population tilted in favor of the less advanced in years? Let's put aside the arguments for or against America's fascination with the youth culture. This has nothing to do with that. This argument is more a disinclination toward growing old, those who have done so, taking care of our burgeoning elderly population, and the ennui of watching life pass by and rigor mortis set in, after one's peak, and while still being above ground. A spectator at one's own post-mortem is never ideal.

Others may say that is not their idea of old age, but that essentially should not matter as the elderly do not get to weigh in on this crucial issue. America's youth who disagree simply need further education upon the horrors of the final countdown. The elderly possibly have more of a stake in the matter; therefore, they cannot be expected to view the issue with clear, cataract-free eyes and rapier reason. We don't vote to strip them of their licenses; we vote so we can avoid for them the embarrassment of this ever happening. Such enactment of law would be kind and beneficent to all.

We are presently a very old population in general, and millions more of the baby boomers will come online and add to the burdensome elderly ranks in a matter of a few short years. The baby boomer generation, perhaps the most dominant generation of late and certainly the beginning of the uptick in population mismanagement, was also not an auspicious one. Its claims to fame reside with two courses of action. It blew things up and sold things, or sold things with which to blow things up, all expertly accomplished, and both well-developed facets of this particular generation that no one needed for the most part. It had minor notable achievements as all generations do, but these noteworthy acts were accomplished mostly by the under 60 set.

Future generations are sure to be much dumber and less effective at everything, unless you consider being led like cattle to the slaughter something necessary and important. Speaking of cattle, the euthanasia of our non-youths could stem the growing tide of our impending food shortage. We might even be able to do away entirely with GMOs. Imagine a world, or at least an America, free of Monsanto, where a tomato tastes like a tomato, and has not been spliced at the genetic level and induced with hundreds of chemicals. Get rid of the flotsam and the jetsam of our elders and this, among much more, are attainable dreams. Possibly, land and goods might become very cheap again. We can pick of the succulent fruits of the trees of our neighbors without the gossipy old lady down the street informing on us.

Nana, the symbolic grandmother, mother, favorite aunt to all of us could provide for all of us long after she goes on to the great beyond. What might be the new opportunities for recycling and cuisine provided by Nana? Nana burgers and Nana nuggets come to mind. Nana treats for our pets. Nana banana ice cream. Nana premium brand fertilizer. Renewable Nan-o energy. The mind staggers at the marketing possibilities. America can restore its noble freedoms. No more will we tolerate the starving elderly populations here in the U.S., and no one eats ignominiously from cat food tins. This is the epitome of the American dream. It can be a reality.

Forget the petty annoyances as well. Never again will we suffer that great rush to get out of the way of some senior in front of us at the grocery store who has suddenly stopped toddling along for no reason. Nor will there exist such long lines for breakfast at McDonald's or Piccadilly on Sunday mornings. Not a single pedestrian will take a millennium to cross the street. Please ask yourself something. Do you really want to open every wine and water bottle for an unappreciative "ageling," change Depends ad nauseum, and chauffeur Nana to the hair stylist twice a week? She might be kind of sweet, albeit slightly demented, but it is likely her room smells bad and Fox News plays incessantly. Such a piece of legislation can have many winning ways. It would be like term limits for Congress. You get in, you make your mark, and you check out.

But perhaps 60 is too arbitrary an age. Maybe 62 is better. There is no great loss on a personal level. The retirement years are highly overrated. Obese, arthritic, with chronic back pain, waking up with "knobly" knees, dehydrated, lacking mobility, COPD, stumbling, blind and bleary-eyed for coffee...you get the unsavory picture. There could be exceptions, for say, those engaged in important medical, military, or technological research. Certain entertainers could live on briefly. If one is still commanding the box office, he or she could keep the curtains up, so to speak. Any number of exceptions could be made. Perhaps a fluid, cogent essay is all that might be required. "Why I should not be Cast into the Mix for Puppy Chow" by Nana Q. Dunsel. And while it may sound like a very good idea to get rid of many of the captains of industry, most of whom fall into this advanced age bracket already, it probably really is not such a stupendous idea. Our business leaders employ a vast number of the more youthful. Think of it.

There might be full employment. Every citizen would produce: working, engaging in commerce, earning his keep. It staggers the mind to believe we could abolish such a blight and burden in our communities. Those that have already attained this particular age of reference could be grandfathered in as well. Loopholes, like nooses, can always be tightened later.

This notion is somewhat new in our culture. It requires a moment or two of adjustment and pause. Perhaps our attitude of sentimentality must be examined. It may even seem abhorrent to many, but a number of cultures have practiced all manner of acts similar to this. From infanticide to simply letting the elderly drift out to sea on a snow patch; one either chews the blubber or the blubber chews him. Life ultimately comes down to natural selection anyway, but in this day of modern medicine and genetic manipulation, we might need to give natural selection a boost.

The elderly folks here in the States, though admirable in many fine ways, should simply be encouraged to go to the great beyond. All sorts of interesting rituals might usher forth. It really is an adventure. After sitting comfortably in their rockers on their front porches, finished with their Texas Toast and pudding, their shawl or blanket clutched to their breast, they could evacuate and leave the task of living to the rest of us. Our families could all get together and rally by their side, as we would know the exact hour of Nana's ultimate success. It could take a lot of guess work out of preparing wills. Along those lines, life insurance would remain in force for the younger members of our society that prematurely conclude their activities. One would also know the exact date of his or her inheritance. Most athletes will tell you as well that it is better to go out at the top of your game. Why not homer every day until the end? Perhaps knowing when you are going to be sent on will help many to lead fuller, richer lives.

Of course, if you do not agree with the law, you may leave for another country. Barbaric states surely will exist outside the U.S. Such a law might be an answer to our nation's immigration problems. There are, in addition, numerous places to retire on a shoestring budget, but don't expect Social Security benefits, as that is an entitlement program that won't have any more entitled. Survivor's benefits could still be paid, and that is always a modest amount at present, so monies paid out would not overwhelm revenues paid in. The amount could change, however. The government should still collect fees for Social Security, at a greatly reduced rate, and use them for paying for survivors' college funds, paying off their homes, and any number of things. The elderly would be performing a service for the rest of the population. Imagine the glory of such self-sacrifice. Lowering taxes, reducing the costs of college and homeownership, making healthcare speedier and more affordable, and perhaps free dental would prove a legacy not soon forgotten. Free dental might not be a crucial element of the plan as one's teeth don't usually go south till the moonlight years. Perhaps, freeing up the mass transit system could be realized instead.

Florida, for example, would no longer need be a place where thousands upon thousands go to die each year. The lemmings destined to bolt finally over the edge could stay put for a reasonable time. Think of the reduction in traffic consternation in cities. It would be a joy to drive a car again unfettered by vehicles that come to a complete halt a mile before a red light. Being cut off while navigating the mean streets by Nana who can't see over her steering wheel would be a distant, murky memory.

"Nana Q. Dunsel, this voice in your head that you are presently hearing is authentic and originates from the United States Government. This is an official transmission. Please rest assured this is not a hoax. Your microchip placed in your brain will activate in precisely two hours. All your bodily functions will cease. Thank you for being an outstanding citizen of our great republic. Future generations will applaud your efforts."

So long, Nana. It was real.

#######

The Runaway Dominatrix
by
Cameron H. Chambers

This is dedicated, in part, to the memory of my former doctor and close friend Dr. R. Taylor King. This story was in no way inspired by him and not the type of classical literature he read, but, while writing a passage in this work, I remembered all that he had done for me in my life, and I wanted to give a word of appreciation. He was a great doctor, a great man, and a great friend. Also, I must mention again a woman who was much more of a direct inspiration for this short work. Christina may you always be well. I will always remember and think of you fondly...

And the first rude sketch that the world had seen was joy to his might heart, till the Devil whispered behind the leaves "It's pretty, but is it art?"

Rudyard Kipling

Prologue

She had had enough. It was time to leave. She was going. The day before was her fifteenth birthday, but she was already built like a woman albeit with a child's perspective. She had packed her backpack and a carry-on, and she slipped downstairs silently to the waiting car. Her boyfriend of six months, a lifeguard named Brad, was taking her to the Greyhound Station. Her parents owned a house on the Atlantic Ocean just north of St. Augustine, Florida. She was departing to Miami. For good.

She climbed in the car. Brad handed Stacey an envelope. "There's a $240 in there. Your ticket is $140. It's all I got," he said.

"Go," she said. He headed out of the neighborhood. He had parked three doors down, so no one would see him. It was four am. "The bus leaves at five," he said. "You're sure you want to do this?"

"I'm sure."

"My sister will pick you up at the bus terminal. She knows some college dudes looking for a roommate. She'll take you there."

"That's perfect," Stacey said. "Thanks."

"What do you think your dad will do?" Brad asked.

"I don't give a fuck about him...that piece of shit. By the time he wakes up, I'll be gone, and he won't be able to touch me again."

"Are you sure you wouldn't rather go to the Police. I'll go in with you. This way you are on your own," Brad said.

"No cops. My mom has had one heart attack already. I don't think she can take the strain. Plus, he would lie and weasel out. He always does. And he has money. Rich men don't go to prison. I'll be all right." Stacey kissed Brad and climbed out of the car. They had arrived at the bus depot. Brad drove off. He could not be seen with her. He was aiding and abetting a minor to run away, and he was aware of the consequences, even if Stacey was not fully cognizant of what she was getting herself into. He loved her. He felt duty bound. She was his first lover though he was nearly eighteen.

Chapter One

Stacey handed her one bag over to the driver of the Greyhound and climbed in with the other one firmly in hand. She looked around and headed to the back of the bus. There was a middle-aged man back there sitting alone. She felt he would do fine.

"May I sit next to you? I get a little scared on trips by myself."

"Sure. Would you like the aisle or window?" he asked.

"You take the window," she said.

The bus loaded up just the slightest bit. There were not too many passengers at this time of morning. Mostly the people looked sleepy and gravitated toward the front and middle of the bus. That suited Stacey fine.

"Where you headed?" she asked.

"Orlando," the man said.

"Nice, I love Orlando. I am going to Tampa." She was, in fact, going to Miami, but did not want anyone other than Brad to know. Her parents did not know about Brad, so he was not a likely suspect to be grilled, interrogated, and broken down. She inched closer to the man. He looked about forty or forty-five, and Stacey figured he had some cash on him. "Once the bus is rolling fairly well, would you like a blowjob?"

"How much?"

She smiled. "Twenty."

"Yeah," he said. The price was right. He handed over a twenty dollar bill.

Stacey was a very good looking girl, short though, about five feet two inches. She had large breasts and easily wore a 36 C bra. She was third generation Italian on her mother's side, and had deep brown eyes that were very expressive, and copious brown hair, which on this day was pulled back off her face in two pig tails with red velvet scrunchies, holding them in place. She had creamy, olive skin that exuded a healthy glow and looked magical to touch. Her scent was enchanting, Pure Seduction by Victoria's Secrets, sweet with a little musky aroma that men remembered. Her brown eyes had the mark of a child's wonder in them, but when Stacey was all business they lit up with scorn or anger, or even joy, if that suited the occasion more precisely. She wept sometimes, mostly for her deceased sister.

Stacey's nose had a gold stud through her left nostril. Her top was a revealing white wrap-around that showed ample cleavage and exposed a smooth back and delicate shoulders. It zipped up above her navel. She wore her breasts speckled in gold glitter. She had no tattoos. The top showed off her belly button, which was also pierced with a silver stud and had hanging from it a one carat diamond. Her jeans were Donna Karan, DKNY, and her brown leather sandals with four inch heels were from Nordstrom. Even in four inch heels she appeared short and voluptuous. Her thighs had just a slight thickness to them, and this made her bottom round and inviting. Her lips were pouty and painted bright red.

Stacey wore a Cartier watch encrusted with diamonds and with a 24K gold band. It had been a gift from her father. She would pawn it if she had to. She had on a 1.2 carat diamond ring with a white gold band from Tiffany's on her right hand. She wore gold feather earrings with a gold locket around her neck that held her only photo of her departed older sister. The locket dropped deliciously into her cleavage. She had loved her older sister very much. Her older sister had hung herself from a living room rafter. Stacey had found her. Stacey believed he touched her too. She had her make-up applied expertly, and she pulled a copy of Nabakov's Lolita from her Gucci bag and placed it in her lap.

The bus rumbled onto the expressway. She figured if they were caught, the bus driver would not throw them off the bus on the expressway. She said, "ready?" to the man.

"Yeah."

She scooted down on the floor of the bus in her jeans in front of the man and unzipped the man's pants and took out his penis. She was grateful it was not a large one. It was a good price he was getting, so she would only do a so-so job. He came quickly anyway. It apparently had been some time for the man. She sucked up the last of his cum and swallowed, asking the man for a drink of his coke. He gave it to her.

"How was that?" she asked.

"Nice. Thank you."

"You're welcome. I aim to please."

"By the way, how old are you?" The johns always asked that question afterwards.

"I am nineteen." Stacey could easily pass for nineteen or twenty.

"Oh, okay, good."

"Do you want to fuck? $50," she said.

"Give me a minute and let me think about it. Do you have any diseases?"

"No, I am clean. What about you?"

No STDs," he said. "Yeah, we can fuck, and I'll even buy you lunch in Orlando."

"Okay."

The man handed her two twenties and a ten this time. She took his dick out of his pants and began stroking it with her right hand to get it hard. He bounced back quickly and was ready to go again. She slipped her Donna Karan's down to her knees and pulled her white thong panties down with them, and she got on the man's lap, reverse cowgirl. She bounced up and down on him for a time. She grabbed his balls with her hand and gave them a firm squeeze. Then she started moving her hips side to side, grinding him a little as he was getting ready to climax, and he made one moan and came. She went down on him and cleaned him up, zipped his fly, and pulled up her jeans.

The bus driver either had not noticed or did not care. Now Stacey had an extra $70, bringing her total to $170 cash that she had on her. There had not been time to empty her bank accounts, but she had checks and credit cards. Little did she realize at the time, she should not use them. The bus pulled into Orlando, and true to his word the man bought Stacey lunch at Taco Bell inside the Greyhound terminal. He then departed out one of the exits. She got back on the bus after lunch and began reading her book.

She had the facial expressions of a woman. Stacey's face did not have that vapid look of a young teenage girl. Her lips were turned down just a fraction, and the light in her eye was a little duller than used it to be, but her face and body were exquisite with a button hook nose, small and cute, and eyebrows perfectly measured to show scorn or distress when she wanted her way. Her face was very expressive; it could look cool as a river of ice or she could plead soulfully with her eyes. She possessed no lines of aging or crows' feet, and she had a confident saunter when she walked. Her butt moved up and down rhythmically as her hips swayed side to side. She knew she could entice any man.

Stacey had changed buses in Orlando after lunch and headed for downtown Miami. It would be about another four hours of riding including stops. She was hoping the college boys would let her stay for free at least for a time. She did not have much money. She figured her father would cancel her credit cards, so she planned on taking huge cash advances on them before he did. He always paid off her balances every month, and her line of credit on the cards was as much as $20,000. She was used to handling large amounts of cash. It didn't scare her. She had her whip and her taser in her backpack, and she knew how to use them.

The bus finally pulled into Miami. It suddenly dawned on Stacey she did not have a clue what Brad's sister looked like, or if she even would be there. Stacey grabbed her checked bag from the driver. The terminal was crowded and dirty. A young woman, about college age, approached Stacey. She held a photo of Stacey in her hands.

"Is this you?" she asked Stacey.

Stacey had not seen her creep up from behind. She looked at the photo. She barely recognized herself from six months earlier. "Yes. Are you Brad's sister?" She didn't need to know her name. Stacey was not trying to get anyone in trouble if it came down to that.

"Yes. I am going to take you near the University of Miami to some apartments. We have to go to Coral Gables. There are some guys you can hang out with. Ready?"

"Yeah."

The two did not speak that much. Brad's sister made a little small chit-chat. "First time in Miami?"

"No, my father brought me here when I was a girl. He and I traveled together a lot. I stayed at a hotel that had a petting zoo. We were on our way to the Keys to go deep sea fishing. What are these boys like?"

"Typical male college students. Dumb and horny."

"Good," Stacey said. She could apply her craft. Stacey was a dominatrix by trade. She had earned money as such since she was twelve years old.
That was a year after her father started molesting her. She had developed early. Her first period was at age ten. She routinely charged $200 per hour, and if the john wanted sex with her, it was $300 per hour. They always wanted sex. She even kissed. It was easy enough to divorce herself from the men who paid for her body. They were all scum.

Brad's sister pulled into the Fountain Lakes Apartments. There was a nice looking fountain in the courtyard. A good landmark for the johns, Stacey thought.

"It is 2G, upstairs. Someone is home. I called. They know you are coming."

"Okay, thanks. I guess this is goodbye. Tell Brad I love him." It wasn't true, but no one needed to know that but Stacey. She climbed the stairs and knocked on the door of apartment 2G.

A young man around age twenty answered the door. He looked at Stacey, and turned to his two friends on the couch, and said, "Who ordered the girl?"

A chubby man, also about age twenty, asked, "Does she have a pizza?"

"No, silly, I am your new roommate."

"The third boy called out, "Stacey?"

"Yes, that's me. She had already entered the living room, where the three boys were playing a retro video game. "GoldenEye?" Stacey asked.

"You know this game?" one of them said. "We can use a fourth."

"I own this game. You'll be sucking my ass in an hour," Stacey said. "Speaking of, can someone give me a ride to the bank later. I'm out of cash."

"Sluggo has a car."

"Which one of you is Sluggo?" Stacey asked.

"I am," the chubby boy sitting next to Stacey said. "I'll give you a ride."

"Thanks. They call you Sluggo because you have a glandular problem?"

"I am just big boned."

"Big bones are nice," Stacey said.

"You're going to fit in around here just fine, Stacey," one of the boys said.

"Maybe if I can get some cash, I'll pick up a couple of large pizzas and a bottle. What does everyone drink?" Stacey said.

"Rum...and can you get some coke?"

"I hope you mean to mix with the rum," Stacey said.

"I do. Rodger has a piss test tomorrow before work. Sluggo knows where to go."

"So that's Sluggo, Rodger and who might you be?" Stacey said.

"I am Lonnie...I am the artist. I play guitar."

"Cool, I play piano. My dad forced me to get lessons for seven years," Stacey said. "I hated it, but I got pretty good. So, Sluggo, I hope, is not your real name."

"Hiram," the chubby boy said.

"Are you Jewish?" Stacey asked. The other boys laughed.

"No."

"Who names their kid Hiram, except a Jew?" Stacey asked.

"My parents."

"Sluggo comes from a real fucked up family. Mom is a meth head, dad's a repeat offender, two dead brothers from overdose."

"I got an f-upped family too, Hiram," Stacey said. "I feel ya."

"Oh!" All three of the boys cried out in unison. Stacey out-maneuvered the deadly tiled entry way, picked up the golden gun, and put a bullet in each player's head.

"I told you, you will be sucking my ass in an hour. No one has ever beaten me. Let's pause. I can use a stretch. I've been on a bus all day."

"I'll show you your room," Lonnie said. He wore the uniform of the college student, jeans with slits at the knees and a skin tight top that showed off large, firm pectoral muscles and nicely shaped biceps. His hair was curly and brown, and he wore a silver cross of St. Peter around his neck. Stacey grabbed her two bags she had deposited at the front door and followed Lonnie into her room. It had a bed with a yellow comforter, desk and chair, and two windows, as hers was a corner room. She and Lonnie would share a bathroom, and the other boys would share one.

"Tell Hiram I'll be ready to go in fifteen minutes, please." Lonnie went out into the hall and shut the door behind him. He knew a girl needs her privacy. Stacey pulled out her diary and lay it on the desk, and she found a pen in her purse and placed it on top. She would write tonight after eating and a few drinks. She had named her diary Susan after her deceased sister, and entered each letter as Dear Susan. She slipped her taser into her purse and used the bathroom. She walked back into the living room. "Ready?" she said.

"Sure," Hiram said. "Let me get my driver's license. Miami cops are a bear. Worse than Georgia cops. What bank do you need to go to?"

"Bank of America," Stacey said.

"Good, that's close by. We'll be back in about an hour, guys."

"An hour?" Stacey asked.

"Welcome to the big city. It takes an hour to go anywhere here."

"Pizza Hut has two large supreme pizzas for twenty bucks," Rodger said. Stacey and Sluggo walked outside, beyond the fountain, and climbed in his Honda Civic. He turned down Memorial Drive.

"We'll go right past the main gate to the University of Miami," Sluggo said. "The bank is up here on the right. We can get a couple of two liters at the Pizza Hut. Otherwise, it's a hike to the convenience store. There's a liquor store by the apartments. Sluggo pulled in the bank parking lot. "Are you going in?"

"Yeah, I shouldn't be too long," Stacey said. Stacey got in line and took a cash advance on three credit cards totaling twenty thousand dollars. The teller asked her a few questions and made a call to the various credit card companies. Just then Stacey thought she might be making a huge mistake. What if they traced the transactions? She was less than two miles from her apartment. The teller handed over the cash in one hundred dollar bills as Stacey had asked for it. She then asked for five twenties for a hundred. He exchanged them. Stacey had a sinking feeling as she exited the bank. Her dad was probably looking for her by now, and she had just blown her cover. All in the same day. She would spend the night and then look for a new place to stay. Tomorrow was Tuesday. The boys would be in classes and Roger would be at work, and she could slip out, possibly out of town. She might buy a car at one of these buy here, pay here lots. She only had a learner's permit, but she doubted they would ask any questions, especially if she was paying in cash.

They returned to the apartment with the pizzas and rum, and Stacey had a couple of drinks with the boys, and a few slices of pizza, and then begged off from further socializing and said she was going to shower and turn in. She wanted to write Susan. It had been her mom's idea to write her departed sister during one of Stacey's worse depressions, and Stacey thought it was a good one. She started a new entry...

Dear Susan,

I am feeling a little bit overwhelmed. I miss you and mom so much. I left home. Where I will end up is anyone's guess. I hope not in a dumpster in some alley. I know I have hurt mom, and I wish I could call, but I can't. She is probably crying right now, and it is all because of me. I feel so evil, like I hurt everyone I know, but it is because of him. He did this to me. I hope he rots in Hell. Well, I should sleep now. I have to move on tomorrow. I know dad is looking for me. He won't let his finest possession go without a bitter fight. I love you always, Susan...Stacey.

Before falling asleep, Stacey slipped her taser under her pillow and put her whip on the nightstand next to her bed. Her taser could bring down a buffalo, and she could whip a man up to ten feet away. She was so good with it, she could get the whip to curl around a man's neck and choke him as she jerked it downward very hard and cut off his breathing. She could knock the wind out of someone much larger than herself in the process. And she had other toys in her bags. Handcuffs, floggers, strap-on dildos of various sizes, vibrators, a silver water dish, a collar and leash, silk ropes,...all these items made for some interesting encounters and very lucrative ones. Her services were always in demand. The price was negotiable sometimes, but it was often steep. Stacey had made as much $5,000 at a bachelor party once. She had sex with the groom-to-be twice and several of the best man's friends. And they never suspected she was fourteen at the time.

Chapter Two

A Mercedes CLK convertible, silver with black leather interior, pulled onto the school grounds. The car twisted around a dirt road to the security shack in back, where the school security officer lived. It was after school hours. The shack was a dusty, beat up trailer that the school loaned out to a has-been private investigator and ex-cop, who now watched the traffic come and go on school grounds and inspected lockers in case there was a problem. But this has-been had come to the attention of a very powerful man. The man was an investment banker and stock broker, and he moved a lot of money around Wall Street for his high roller clients, very successfully as well. He would be missed if he did not show up to work; this has-been private investigator could disappear for a thousand Sundays, and no one would ever be the wiser. But then one of three ex-wives he owed alimony or child support to might cry foul. Even the lowliest have supporters, especially if he owes funds.

The man stepped out of his sports car, dressed in a black jacket, black slacks and white Polo, and matching black leather belt. He looked in his late forties; he could beam a bright smile that he turned off and on when needed to get what he wanted, and had a slightly receding hairline. His teeth were straight and pearly. He was fit and tan, owing to his three mile jog on the beach each morning around sun-up. As was his routine, he then showered and climbed into his car and went to his office seven days a week, sometimes staying as late as midnight. He owned an investment firm that he had started with just one client, a millionaire ball player, who had not a clue about investing on Wall Street, but had the good sense to hire someone who could turn his few short years in the pros into millions of dollars. Soon, other clients followed, and the man in the black jacket was making seven figures a year and had thirteen people working for him, most of them other brokers.

He was a bold man and possessed a strength of character to the point of being domineering and controlling. He never let others decide for him, not even his wife, who over the years he had worn down into complete submission. He had a reputation of being ruthless, and that of a clever man who could read stock trends. In the 90s he had made his fortune and the fortunes of his clients in the dot com start-ups, and had bailed on them just in time, reaping huge profits. He had a proposition for the ex-private investigator and would not be turned away. He would have his only surviving child returned to him by the following weekend. He had gone through her panty drawer the morning after she left, and seen she had emptied it. He knew she had run away.

He banged loudly on the trailer door. The has-been was watching re-runs of Cheers. He answered the door.

"Mr. Formelli? Mario Formelli?" the man in the black leather jacket asked.

"Yeah, but I don't have any money, so if you are going to arrest me, just let me get my medication. Then Formelli saw the convertible. "What's this about?"

"Would you like to make some money? I assure you it is legit."

"That got me three years in a federal pen the last time I heard those words."

"Oh, I see. I wondered why the fall from grace. An associate told me you are a good tracker, and my teenage daughter has run away, and I would like her returned."

"What if she doesn't want to come back?"

"It's up to you to bring her back. Restraints are permissible. There's two thousand in this envelope, and I'll give you another two thousand if you have her back to me by this weekend. Here's a recent photo, here's the address of an ATM at a bank where she removed some money yesterday. She's probably still near there."

"Yeah, maybe. Pretty girl. How old is she? I also need five hundred per day."

"Done. Fifteen."

"How do I know this is your daughter, and not some eye witness to a murder?"

"Here is her birth certificate, and here is my driver's license. Note the name of the father, Ron Whitaker. My daughter's name is Stacey Whitaker."

"Okay, I'll do it. Does she have any visible markings?"

"No tattoos. Her nose is pierced and her belly button is pierced. She wears halter tops a lot. Here's my cell phone number. Keep me posted. Give me your number," Whitaker said.

"I don't have one, but I'll get one and call you with the number," Formelli said.

"How soon can you leave? She left yesterday morning I am

guessing. I was at work until late, and my wife is traveling. I prefer not to involve the police. They are too inept."

"A half hour," Formelli said. "The first forty-eight hours are crucial. She probably had a connection in Miami, but they may be moving on from there. It could even be internationally. How much money did she take?"

"Two grand," Whitaker lied. He knew the amount. The bank had informed him.

"Why me?" Formelli said.

"I heard you were the best in the business once. Here's your chance to regain some of your dignity."

"I'm more interested in the money. All right, the sooner you leave, the sooner I can leave."

Whitaker said, "call me," and sped off down the dusty, dirty lane in his Mercedes.

Formelli packed an overnight bag. A change of socks and underwear, a t-shirt and another pair of jeans. And handcuffs. He guessed he did not need his ankle cuffs for a fifteen year old girl. Formelli packed his medication. He had a heart problem at age fifty, and he had a touch of high blood pressure, both regulated well with pills that he took every morning. He took blood thinners, and they could make him dizzy if he did not eat. He also had a drinking problem but was not an around-the-clock drinker. He then packed his 9mm Glock, policeman's issue.

Now that he was a felon, it was illegal for him to have this gun, but he figured he could always claim it was not his. It had been filed and was untraceable. Furthermore, it was stolen, and he knew for a fact that it had not been reported stolen. Most gun owners don't report the theft of their guns as they should.

Formelli locked his trailer, climbed into his pick-up, and drove off toward I-95 South. It was nine am Tuesday morning. With any luck he would be in Miami by two pm. He wanted to find this girl by nightfall, cuff her, stuff her, and get his money. He would take her to a hotel near Jacksonville, Florida or one of the beaches like Ponte Vedra and call her dad to bring the money and come get her. He did not trust her dad. Men with money cannot be trusted.

He didn't have a meeting with his probation officer until the next day. He hoped to wrap up his business the same night before. His probation officer would never know he left the city. She was a nasty, racist black woman with a big fat ass and droopy tits she always rested on her desk, but he had to put up with her. She got his case, and that is where his case and his "sorry ass," as she commented frequently, remained. It sounded to Formelli like she called him a cracker under her breath sometimes. She hated him, and he hated her, and he hated the whole legal system, which he had been a huge part of for years. Then he had seen it from a different viewpoint. His most recent point of view had changed him.

The house phone rang. Stacey answered, but did not say anything. The caller asked for Roger. "He's not here. He has work today," Stacey said.

"Shit," the caller said. It was the voice of a young man. "We were supposed to hang out. Now I got nothing to do."

"You can come over here and hang out with me. What's your name?"

"Mike," he said.

"Mike, you wanna party with me? I am their new roommate and I am gorgeous, and I am looking to get laid, but it will cost you."

"How much?"

"One hundred." Stacey knew it was a lot for a young man who was probably out of work or a college student, but the University of Miami is a private school, and the kids that attended came from money. She guessed Roger and maybe Mike had bad grades or were on academic probation or had flunked out and rather than return home had gotten jobs. Roger worked construction, which was very slow in the Miami area at the time. Builders had overbuilt condos and they were going for a song during this most recent recession.

"I've only got fifty," Mike said. Everyone low-balled in a bad economy.

"For fifty, I'll tie you up and spank you, and then jack you off. How's that?"

"How about head?"

"Okay, but I spank really hard. I am a professional dominatrix. When you come inside the door, get down on your knees, and I am going to handcuff you. And don't be one minute late, Mike, or I will punish you. Got it?"

"Yes ma'am. I have a couple of things to do first. Is it alright ma'am if I come over around three?"

"Since you asked politely, yes. I'll make it worth your time, so bring some extra cash to tip me. You won't be disappointed."

"Yes ma'am. See you at three," and Mike hung up. Stacey had slept till noon. She had the dream again. She guessed she needed the rest, even though her sleep was a fitful one. It had been an emotional day the day before. She thought to write Susan, but her habit was to write at night, often late into the night, so instead she decided to get ready for her rendezvous. The dream was always the same. It was of her dead sister hanging from the rafters. After a quick trick, she thought she had better vacate the premises. She was sure her father was looking for her, and she knew how resourceful a man he could be. He might know people in Miami too.

Stacey decided to eat some left over pizza and take a shower. It would take her a while to get ready for her date. She called the johns dates. Stacey had never had a real date with a boy that did not involve a financial transaction. Her father had seen to that. She ate the pizza cold though she had spied a microwave. Left over pizza is meant to be eaten cold and for breakfast. She took off her underwear and bra. She felt good like a woman on her own in her own apartment. She had slept in her bra. Her mother always told her it made for a perkier rack, and her mother was almost forty and her breasts were magnificent. Stacey strolled into the bathroom and flung open the shower curtain. She first turned the water on hot, and she left the door to the bathroom open so the steam would go out.

She felt very good. The dream from last night was startling when it recurred, which it sometimes did. As soon as she realized it was only a dream, she felt better and was able to carry on with her day. The dream drove sleep away, but Stacey wanted to get up anyway. The water had warmed up in the shower, and there was good pressure in the apartment, so Stacey hopped in. She began to scrub down with body wash. She scrubbed her pits first. They were the most in need of attention. She washed her handsome face and smooth breasts. Then she washed her tan creamy stomach, legs and buttocks. She realized she had brought all her toiletries, except she had forgotten a towel. There was one hanging from a hook. She would have to use that. It was probably Lonnie's. She guessed he would not mind, and since she was leaving, she did not really care. She slowly inched her fingers down and first massaged around her clit. She rubbed it with two fingers. It would feel good to have some relief. She thought of naked men lying on the beach. The warm soapy water felt inviting, but, as usual, she almost got to orgasm, but did not. She was not always very vocal during sex or when masturbating, but she let out a stifled cry, a half whimper because she could not come. She then shaved her legs in the shower, even though it was only peach fuzz on them, and she shaved her pussy. She liked to keep it neat.

She brushed her teeth in the shower. It made her feel as though she was getting things done in a timely manner and not playing around like a schoolgirl might be inclined. School was difficult for Stacey. She received good grades, but was a bit of a social outcast. She had few close friends, and no one she could confide in. Brad had not gone to her school. She met him on the beach one day. Stacey was going to enter a grown-up world, more so than she already had, and she needed to have some measure of control over things she had a say about. Brushing her teeth in the shower cut down on the time it took her to get ready for her affairs.

She thought for a moment. Stacey was thinking of getting her GED and going to a college somewhere, but that was plan B. Plan A involved a flight to the French Riviera and finding an apartment and settling down. She had been there before and fallen in love with it. She knew this required cash. More than what she had at present.

Stacey stepped out of the shower. She brushed a towel through her hair and dried off. She applied just the proper amount of hair spray to hold her brown locks in a crinkled, crimpy position. It looked terribly seductive. She poofed it up, so it hung deliciously around her slender neck and taut, sleek shoulders. Mike had no chance against her feminine wiles, she thought to herself. He had better show up. It was time to get dressed. She stepped right into her left boot, which she pulled up to mid-thigh. It was a black leather boot, very expensive, with three inch heels. Years of ballet training, insisted upon by her father, had made Stacey's balance superb. She had also gone in for gymnastics and excelled. She pulled the right boot on from a standing position as well and slid it up over her knee. Her panties were a black thong with silver concentric rings around them worn as a belt. And her bra was a black latex and strapless. She got out her silver water dish and a large vibrator. She always made the johns strip naked and drink water from the bowl while kneeling on the floor.

She got out her whip and her taser in case she had to protect herself. She had gone into a rough situation a time or two, but she was fearless, the mark of a young woman, any adolescent really, but she had always escaped a cruel fate where the johns were concerned. Finally, she was prepared to put on her make-up. She put Smokey Eyes on her eyelids with black mascara. Her eyes were as dark as night. She put on Pure Seduction, a dab on her wrists and on her breasts. She walked into the living room. . She took a chair from the dining table and turned its back to the door and straddled it, so only her face and her boots showed to someone entering the door. Once she stood up, Mike would see her and have no chance. She would toy with him like a spider does a fly. He would obey her every command. If he did not, he got the paddle. And Stacey liked to be obeyed. She demanded it.

Mario Formelli had made his way into Coral Gables. Before finding the specific Bank of America where Stacey took the cash advance, he stopped at a Wal-Mart and bought a cell phone and loaded it with minutes. He also had about thirty color prints of Stacey's photo made. He then found the bank on Ponce de Leon Blvd. He would canvass neighborhoods until there was no one out, knock on doors, talk to anyone he could. It was old-fashioned police work, and he had it in his blood. He could sniff out a lead just like a hound and follow it to a logical conclusion. He knew she was staying somewhere close by. He knew she had to eat. He knew she had a couple thousand dollars or so he thought. There was a municipal airport not too far away and Miami International. He would have to call limo services, cab companies, and he would have to do it all himself. Stacey could not very well pay for a flight with cash. That usually took a credit card, but Formelli knew how resourceful these runaways could be. She might have a card or two in her name that her father did not know about. Formelli tried to think whom Stacey might be meeting. Surely, it was a boy. Then he realized the University of Miami was in Coral Gables and decided to go there next. It was close to the branch bank where Stacey had transacted business the day before. She was staying near here. Formelli could feel it.

There was a knock at the door of apartment 2G. Stacey thought to herself, "it's show time." It was time to make some money. She was glad to be working again.

"Come in," Stacey said. The john entered the room. "Take off your clothes and get down on your knees." The john followed orders. He had had previous training, which always made Stacey's job easier.

"Is anyone here?" Mike asked.

"Shut up. You will speak only when spoken to. Throw your wallet over here. Fifty. Okay." Stacey got up from the chair. She rose up slowly and dramatically, so the john could take her in fully.

"My god, you're beautiful," Mike gushed. Stacey walked behind him, riding crop in hand, and pulled his arms behind him and handcuffed him. "We are going to have a little fun, Mikey...do you want to play with me?"

"Yes," the boy gushed again.

"Good. Are you going to be an obedient slave? You might get a prize."

"Yes ma'am."

"Call me Mistress Dominique. Lick the heel of my boot, slave." The john performed his duty. Stacey sat on the couch as her slave sat on the floor on his folded legs underneath him, leaning over to lick her boots, and she hit him with the riding crop rather forcefully on his back and behind. He moaned in discomfort each time he was struck and this made Stacey whip the boy harder. She placed the heel of her boot in the boy's mouth, and said, "suck." He did. The john was a gangly boy, tall and skinny, and not much more than nineteen. Stacey got up from the couch and got the leather flogger. She had the john bend over the couch, and she inspected his ass as she slapped it with the flogger. She stuck her finger in. She then reached around and began to fondle Mike's dick. It was rock hard. She squeezed his balls, and he let out a bit of a yelp.

"Calm down, slave. I won't hurt you too badly," Mistress Dominique said. She began rubbing on her slave's penis, as she slapped his ass. She took off her bra and leaned into Mike from behind him, putting her breasts into his back. His body tensed, shuddered and then he came.

"Did I say you could cum, slave?" Stacey's voice was stern.

"No, Mistress Dominique."

"Very bad. You have been naughty. Now I have to use my strap-on dildo on you." Stacey told the john to stay in that position, and she got into her strap-on. She lubricated his ass with KY jelly, and slid the nine inch strap-on deep inside the boy. He cried out and tried to turn around, but Stacey could out maneuver him easily since he was handcuffed. She pushed him back around and down over the couch and pressed her tits into his back again, and the boy settled down. She started tearing up his hole. She thrust very strongly almost lifting the boy off his feet. She would pull him back down with his handcuffed wrists, which hurt the boy terribly. And then she would thrust some more and pull his hair. She bit him hard on his shoulder.

"Do you have more cash for your Mistress?"

"In my socks, please stop."

"Okay, good slave. She pulled out the strap-on and turned the boy around and planted a kiss on his mouth. He opened his mouth and they kissed more. She took off his handcuffs and put them back on with his hands in front of him. "Sit on the couch." He obeyed. Stacey went to his socks on the floor and pulled out another hundred in twenties and stuffed the money inside her panties with the other fifty dollars. "Okay," she said. "I am going to give you the best head you have ever had." She kneeled down to the boy's cock and took it in her mouth and began stroking it with her right hand and tongue. He moaned in pleasure. She sucked and bit his penis and sucked on his balls. He used his handcuffed hands, which were now in front of him, to press down on Stacey's head as she sucked his dick. It was a bold move for a slave, but Stacey did not resist. He then came in her mouth and she swallowed.

Stacey got up from her position on the floor. She said, "I think you need a drink of water." She got the water bowl and placed some water from the tap in it. She put it down on the floor and said, "drink." The john slid down to the carpeted floor and did as he was commanded. Stacey rested her boots on his back. "Give me your mobile number, slave," she said. "We can play again, but it won't be here."

Mario Formelli had pulled up to Fountain Grove Apartments. He went inside the leasing office. He asked the lady there if she had seen this person, showing her a photo of Stacey, and explained he was an officer from the Jacksonville Sherriff's Office looking for a teen runaway. He flashed a fake badge. She had not seen her, but it was rent day, and several people were up at the office paying their rent. One boy said he might have seen her last night. Formelli asked which apartment, but the boy wasn't sure, but he thought he saw her go in a second floor apartment. Formelli asked which building and the boy pointed to the building, which was near the leasing office.

Formelli parked his pick-up in the lot under apartment 2G. He walked up the stairs. He had his throwaway strapped to his left ankle. Every cop worth his salt carries a throwaway pistol.

He pulled his Glock and burst in the door. He pointed it right at the braless Stacey, and said, "get your things...you're going home." The young man on the floor next to Stacey rose up and ran out the door screaming for his life. He was naked and cuffed, but he figured it would be better than getting shot.

"Who hired you?" Stacey commanded.

"Your father. Get dressed."

"What's his name?" Stacey had not budged an inch off the couch. She did not try to cover her breasts.

"Ron Whitaker. Now, am I going to have cuff you?"

"No, I'll get my things." He had the drop on Stacey. There was nothing she could do. She thought about tasing him, but she would save that till later. She put on her street clothes in the bedroom. Formelli had followed her in there. He drooled a little as Stacey put on her clothes, wiping a small bit of spittle from the corner of his mouth. He could tell there was no one else in the apartment. About a five hour drive and he would collect his money. He might have enough left over to pay off his probation officer. How he hated that bitch. He would still have monthly meetings for the next several months, one of which was coming up soon, but at least he would not have to scramble for the $75 each time he met her. He became a little distracted, which is a cardinal sin with routine police affairs. He began to fantasize about this femme fatale as she packed her whip and paddle and floggers.

Chapter Three

Stacey sat in the pickup. She was determined she was not going home, but she had to play her cards right. "Wait for the opportunity," she told herself. Just as her mother had taught her about traffic on a busy street, there is always a break in the pattern when you can go. When it comes, seize it.

"Where are you taking me?" Stacey asked.

"We're going back to Jacksonville first. Then we'll meet with your father."

"Why Jacksonville? What's in Jacksonville?"

"I am taking you to a safe house, so then I can turn you over to your father. No games. You'll be safe with me. No one will hurt you," Formelli said.

"I think you have your shoe on the wrong foot, my friend. I am always the one who inflicts the pain, and if you get caught up running my father's errands for him, you will see."

"You can talk all you want," Formelli said. "The air's free." Formelli pulled out into traffic and started toward I-95. From there it was a straight shot to Jacksonville and a hotel room. He would call Mr. Whitaker and get the rest of his money.

Stacey was silent for a goodish while and then asked, "What's your name?"

"Mario," he said.

"Mario? Mario what?"

"Formelli."

"You're an amico mio? Or are you a goomba?" Stacey said. Her mom had taught her some Italian. She knew French as well.

"Goomba is an insult," Formelli said. "But, yes, I am Italian. Second generation."

"I am third generation on my mom's side. And I know goomba is an insult. My father is American. Americans are either Puritans or perverts. Or both." The pair rode on in silence for some time again.

"Hey, do you know any jokes?" Stacey asked. She wanted to soften him up a little, so he might make a mistake. "Why do all black people have nightmares?" she said.

"I don't know. Why?"

"Because we shot the only one with a dream," Stacey said. Formelli chuckled.

"What do you a call a Mexican without a lawnmower?" Formelli said.

"What?"

"Unemployed." They both chuckled over that one.

"I got one," Stacey said. "Why aren't there any Mexicans on Star Trek?"

"I don't know. Why?" Formelli said.

"Because they don't have jobs in the future either."

"What word begins with n and ends with r that you never want to call a black person?"

"Nigger," Stacey said.

"No, neighbor." Stacey howled with derisive laughter.

"What do you call a nigger chinaman with AIDS?" Stacey said.

"I don't know. What?" Formelli said.

"Coon-die-soon." Formelli howled with laughter.

"What's long and hard on a black man?" Formelli said.

"His cock," Stacey said.

"No, third grade," Formelli said. "You want to get something to eat? I could use a bite."

"Yeah, sure. We passed a billboard for an Olive Garden a mile or two back. It's peasant food, but it will do in a pinch."

"I like the Olive Garden," Formelli said.

"My mom's a much better cook."

"Which exit?" Formelli asked.

"This one, I think," Stacey said. Formelli turned off the interstate. He was hungry. He liked this girl. She was good company for him. He wished she was a little older, and they had met under different circumstances. She certainly was beautiful and just his type. When he was a cop he had gone out with young, pretty girls like Stacey. But now he was a lowly security guard on probation with three ex-wives and four children he had to pay child support for. He made about fifteen thousand a year now, and the court took all but about five. He could barely keep gas in his pick-up. They pulled into the parking lot of the Olive Garden. It was crowded with SUVs and late model cars, Hondas, Camrys, even Beemers and such.

"I don't get to go out very often, so my table manners might not be all that," Formelli said.

"Just eat the pasta like you would eat my pussy and there are no regrets," Stacey said.

"I wish I didn't have to take you back," Formelli said, as he held the door open wide for Stacey. He was pretending they were on a date. She in her little, black Tulane University bottoms and a tank top, and the big old goomba in his old man shorts and sleeveless t-shirt. He noticed everything about her and wondered why she had Tulane University inscribed on her luscious cheeks. He found her at the University of Miami. She must know some college pukes. Her ass looked magnificent in the shorts. He pretended she was in a tiny black dress. At least he wasn't sweating. He could give off a terrible odor when he did. They were seated at their table after not too long of a wait.

"Do you have any idea what you are taking me back to?" Stacey questioned Formelli. "Do you know what my father does to me?"

"What? He takes away your credit card?"

"He rapes me. On a consistent basis whenever he feels like." There was silence. Formelli was thinking. He liked this girl, but he had no way of knowing if what she said was true. He asked why she didn't go to the police. Her answer sounded plausible. But Formelli had witnessed her friend, or whomever it was, handcuffed in the apartment drinking from a water dish with Stacey's legs propped up on him like he was an ottoman for her enjoyment. He had seen what she was wearing. He knew women like that always got their way. And they were not above lying.

Then Formelli started thinking about the money. He could pay off his probation, he could catch up on his child support, maybe even have enough money to take in a ball game with his oldest boy. He decided right then and there it was business between him and Stacey. They could have fun, but the bottom line was he needed that money. He had nothing to say to her. Fortunately, the waiter came. They both ordered the never-ending pasta dishes with meat sauce, breadsticks and salad. The waiter offered Stacey a glass of wine. They both had one. Apparently she looked over twenty-one to the waiter. Time perhaps had aged her a little, but hers was a lithe, fine body, a keen disposing mind, and an invincible spirit.

When Formelli did speak, he asked, "how's the wine?"

"It's foot wash," Stacey said. "How's your pasta?"

"Not too bad, thank you," he said. "I want some more salad. That salad is pretty good. And more pasta."

"Do you ever make it into St. Augustine?" Stacey asked.

"Not too often anymore. Been a million times."

"There's a small pasta joint in the old part of town. Delicious sandwiches for about five bucks. They are huge too. The sandwiches make two meals. When my mom felt better, she and I would go there all the time."

"What's wrong with your mom?"

"What? He takes away your credit card?"

"He rapes me. On a consistent basis whenever he feels like." There was silence. Formelli was thinking. He liked this girl, but he had no way of knowing if what she said was true. He asked why she didn't go to the police. Her answer sounded plausible. But Formelli had witnessed her friend, or whomever it was, handcuffed in the apartment drinking from a water dish with Stacey's legs propped up on him like he was an ottoman for her enjoyment. He had seen what she was wearing. He knew women like that always got their way. And they were not above lying.

Then Formelli started thinking about the money. He could pay off his probation, he could catch up on his child support, maybe even have enough money to take in a ball game with his oldest boy. He decided right then and there it was business between him and Stacey. They could have fun, but the bottom line was he needed that money. He had nothing to say to her. Fortunately, the waiter came. They both ordered the never-ending pasta dishes with meat sauce, breadsticks and salad. The waiter offered Stacey a glass of wine. They both had one. Apparently she looked over twenty-one to the waiter. Time perhaps had aged her a little, but hers was a lithe, fine body, a keen disposing mind, and an invincible spirit.

When Formelli did speak, he asked, "how's the wine?"

"It's foot wash," Stacey said. "How's your pasta?"

"Not too bad, thank you," he said. "I want some more salad. That salad is pretty good. And more pasta."

"Do you ever make it into St. Augustine?" Stacey asked.

"Not too often anymore. Been a million times."

"There's a small pasta joint in the old part of town. Delicious sandwiches for about five bucks. They are huge too. The sandwiches make two meals. When my mom felt better, she and I would go there all the time."

"What's wrong with your mom?"

"She had a heart attack about a year ago. She hasn't recovered all that well. I think my father has been slipping something in her drinks."

"Is he that big of a fucking creep?"

"You don't know the half of it. He wants me all to himself. He murdered my sister, or caused her to commit suicide. He raped her too, but I can't prove it. We were close. She was on the verge of telling me one time, but she burst into tears and walked out of the room. She hid the ugly secret from my mom, but I think my mom suspects about me. See what you are taking me back to?"

"He'll get his. They always do. And I am not a deeply religious man, but I think karma explains a lot. He'll come back as destitute and retarded in a family of no resources."

"Like you," Stacey smiled. "I'll have some more pasta and another glass of foot wash," she told the waiter that Formelli had summoned.

"We have a lovely Chianti," the waiter said.

"We'll both have that," Formelli said. He ignored Stacey's comment from before. "Might as well enjoy your last day of freedom," he said.

They spoke of matters that interested themselves, and Formelli told her he used to be a cop, but had been arrested by a Narcotics agent for purchasing coke. It was not even for him. It was for his wife. She was about twenty years younger than Formelli and had a thousand dollar a week habit. They were going through a divorce at the time. He had also tried to bribe the Narcotics agent. He swore in prison he had gotten the only honest Narco cop in Jacksonville. The judge shipped Formelli off to Coleman, a low security federal pen in south Florida, where he did three years and got out. The sentence had been four years. Stacey was fascinated by the story. She had experimented with pot and coke, but found neither to her liking. She liked wine, and if she wanted something stronger, a sweet Bourbon like Jim Beam and coca-cola suited her.

Formelli paid for the bill after ordering a bottle of the Chianti to take with him. He was far from intoxicated, but he had plans for later on this evening. Stacey accompanied him to his pick-up. She offered to drive, but Formelli refused. She planned to gas up at a convenience store and lose Formelli and take his truck, but he would not fall for that one she saw. "Patience," she thought.

They climbed in the pick-up and were off down the road to Jacksonville again. Eventually, arriving in Jacksonville, Formelli found a seedy little hotel named the Gator Inn. It was $39 for the night. The room smelled of cheap, stale cigarettes and urine, but it looked reasonably clean. He sat at the desk and Stacey unfolded herself on the bed. He dialed Whitaker's number. "I've got her. I am at 6161 Baymeadows Way, just off I-95." He left that message on Whitaker's cell phone. Two minutes later Whitaker called back and said he would be there in about an hour. It was, at the time Formelli placed the call, about nine pm. "He'll be here in an hour or so," he said to Stacey. "What would you like to do?"

"We could fuck," she said. Her cherubic smile gave way to a darker beast inside her.

"Okay," Formelli said. He was hoping she would be interested. She got up from resting on the bed and ripped Formelli's shirt open, the buttons flying off at odd angles and a couple under the bed linens. She pulled out his belt and took down his pants, as he reached over her and undid her bra. She took her top off and lay it and her bra on the side of the bed. She undid her jeans, and slipped them off in one smooth motion, leaving her black lace thong on. Formelli was naked and his manhood was erect, all three inches of it. Stacey wanted to tease him a bit, so she grabbed his dick with her right hand and gave it a tight squeeze. He moaned as a little pre-cum came out of his tip. She went to her bag and placed a blindfold over the eyes of the reluctant man. He was usually not the one in charge in the bedroom. It is often that way with cops. His ex-wives had cracked the whip on his behind many times, and he loved it. So, without too much protestation, he gave into his fifteen year old seductress. She then mounted him and bobbed up and down on him. He came in a flash. She knew he would. She licked him clean, and then lay beside him, waiting for round two.

Formelli apologized. He said it had been a couple of years since he had been laid. Stacey kissed him, and got out of bed and uncorked the wine. She went into the bathroom. Luckily there were a couple of sterile plastic cups. She poured both of the cups full of the wine, and she took the cups back to bed with her and handed one over to Formelli. "My handsome goomba, it is okay. You will do better next time, or I will simply have to beat you."

"Yes, Mistress. Mistress, can I still see you after you go back?"

"Sure you can. I get two hundred an hour."

"You're a call girl?" Formelli asked a little dismayed.

"Drink, my pet. We are having fun now. Let's not ruin it."

"Yes, Mistress."

"Good little goomba." Stacey reached under the covers and began massaging Formelli's cock. He drank down his wine and was ready again. This time Stacey got on top of him facing away, a favorite position of hers, and Formelli had considerably more stamina this round. She bounced up and down on his cock and legs, slapping his balls as she went, telling him to call out her name. He moaned sweetly under his breath, "Stacey, my Goddess, fuck me harder, make me cum again, please, I beg you." Then Stacey cried out, "shit, oh my God!" At first she did not know what was happening. She had never reached orgasm before. Her entire body shuddered and she came, but she hung in there for her handsome man, and they came together. She fell off of him gasping for breath. "I came," she said, as she kissed Formelli all over his face. His whiskers felt raw to her tongue. "You get the wine," she said. "Yes, dear," he said.

Formelli's naked body was still in decent shape. Though he was older and had a little paunch, he clearly had kept up his appearance. He had all his teeth, except one, and there was a hole between one tooth and a back molar on the top right side of his mouth, but it did not show, even when he smiled. He did not have much to smile about in his life lately. He had a fairly full crop of wavy brown hair with just a receding line where he had kept a part for many years. Now he combed it straight back, and it spiked up a hint, especially if he used some gel. He got the wine bottle and returned to bed. He sat up, took a swig from the bottle, and lit a cigarette and smoked it right there in bed. He passed the bottle over to Stacey. She drew a big gulp and handed it back. She fanned the air around her with her hand, protesting his smelly cigarette, but secretly she did not mind that her goomba smoked.

Formelli said, "I am going to catch twenty winks. Don't go anywhere."

"Where can I go?" she said.

Formelli rolled over like a big bear and started snoring in an instant. With his sleep apnea, he fell into a disturbed sleep, light, and without good oxygen to his lungs. Stacey knew this was her chance. She slid gracefully out of bed and got dressed noiselessly. She took her handcuffs out of her bag, making sure they did not clink together and awake the sleeping teddy bear. She then handcuffed one of the cuffs to the bed post, and then artfully wrangled Formelli's wrist into the other. It clanked closed on his thick wrist, and he woke up, demanding to know what was going on.

"You didn't really think I was going to let you take me back?" Stacey asked.

"Get these cuffs off me, God damn it."

Stacey grabbed up Formelli's clothes, first checking that his keys and his wallet were in his pants. She spun toward the door. "It's just business, lover. But we could have been something." She blew him a kiss and walked out and closed the door behind her. She walked down to Formelli's truck, got in and headed down the road, leaving Jacksonville in her rear mirror. She had only a fifteen minute or so jump on her father, but he would not know which way she was going. She knew which way he would be coming and she stuck to the back roads out of town. She got over the bridge, crossing the powerful St. Johns River, and sighed a deep breath of relief. She was on her own again. She was going. It had been a narrow escape. She would have to be more careful, she thought.

Ron Whitaker arrived at the Gator Inn and went upstairs to the room designated on the phone by his hired agent Mario Formelli. He knocked loudly twice. Formelli said, "Come in."

"It's locked."

"Get the front desk to open the door. I'm in a little bit of a pickle."

"Where's my daughter?" Whitaker said.

"Just get someone to open the door."

Whitaker did not know what this latest snafu was, so he did as he was requested though he resented being given an order by a pathetic underling. He couldn't comprehend what Formelli said about being in a pickle. What could go wrong with such simple instructions, he wondered. It was late, he had worked all day and night and just wanted his daughter back and to go home. He went down to the office and told the lady that the man in 7C was in distress and could she open the door. Whitaker explained to the lady that the man was a friend of his. She reluctantly opened the door after getting permission from Formelli. She did not want any police or emergency workers around either, luckily so for Formelli. When she got the door open, she and Whitaker saw Formelli sprawled across the bed, naked, with his right wrist in the air handcuffed to the bed post. His hair was all bedraggled and he was drunk.

Whitaker took one look and said, "You're fired. And I ought to have you locked up again for having sex with my daughter."

"I don't think you want to do that," Formelli said. His tone was threatening and it made Whitaker pause.

Whitaker drove off and went back home. It was a half hour's drive to his beach house, and he needed a shower and something to eat. He would contemplate his next move in the morning.

"Formelli told the night manager that he had been robbed. He would pay for the room, but he didn't have any clothes so he had to wait till someone brought him clothes and money. He also said he did not want to involve the police. The lady uncuffed him. His arm had gone completely numb from being in the same position for an hour. He thanked the lady as he rubbed life back into his arm and told her he would be checking out soon and pay up in full. She was thankful she did not have to call the cops. She had not seen Stacey and did not know she was underage, and it would not have mattered to her anyway. There was no damage to the room. She was glad of that.

Formelli, in his drunken state, could remember only one telephone number, which he called. It was his ex-wife's house. She had his twins. He pleaded with her over the phone and finally cajoled her into bringing him some of his clothes that he still had at her house, a house that had been his before the divorce. She got out of bed, checked that the twins were sleeping, and piled into her beat up Camry from a first marriage and drove to an ATM to pull out forty dollars for Formelli, so he could pay his tab at the hotel. She handed him the money after driving across town in the middle of the night.

"Thanks babe. I owe you one. I am going to catch this crook, and when I get paid I'll take you and the kids to a nice steak dinner."

"Save it. I have heard it all before. Just go pay the hotel. Do you need to be dropped somewhere?"

"Yeah, if you can. Back at my trailer. There's a special place in Heaven for you darling."

"Yeah, God loves fools. That's forty I will never see again. Why were you naked?"

"He got the drop on me and pointed my own gun to my head and made me strip and take off my clothes."

"Aren't you getting a little old to chase bad guys?" Formelli's ex said.

"Maybe, but the money was good, a grand to bring him back

from Miami, but he got away. But I'll get him. He took the money too."

"I didn't even know you were doing bounty hunting."

"I'm not licensed, but that means I don't have to post a bond. I work for someone. This was the first gig, and I guess I messed up."

"Figures. Here we are. All safe and sound. Get a shower, Mario. You smell like drunken crap." Formelli's ex-wife stopped at the entrance to the school grounds, which had a large swinging barricade across it fastened in the middle with a padlock. She let him out, and drove off. She had been a good wife, faithful and loyal, but she had wanted more than he could give. He had worked hard, but he was not educated and people like that always get squeezed out of the work force as they get older. Then too there was the time he spent in the pen. It had taken a toll on their marriage and their boys. She had his twin boys, now aged six years, and Mario had missed some very important years and had had no income he could share with his wife or his sons. So, she divorced him, but finding a suitable mate had not been so easy for her.

Formelli ducked under the barricade and trudged to his trailer. He did need a shower he decided, but he knew he did not have that much time, since he planned on traveling by bus. He called Alex, his former partner, and asked to borrow five hundred dollars. Alex's wife was a mortgage broker, and even in lean times, she had set herself and Alex up well with her own agency, so Alex always had cash and he never turned Mario down. Mario's credit with Alex was good, surprisingly. Alex was another Italian; he had served on the Jacksonville Sheriff's Office for over twenty years, and then been pushed out due to a back injury. It was really because his salary was too high, and the department was faced with cuts every year, as the City of Jacksonville was broke, like most municipalities around the State of Florida. Detroit was just the beginning for a string of American cities. So Alex told Mario he would bring the money by in a couple of hours, and indeed Mario had time for coffee, breakfast and a shower before launching off after this girl. Formelli had a good idea where to look for her.

Chapter Four

One silently stewed at his desk in his office. One drove her new, raggedy pick-up to freedom on I-10. One caught the bus. One felt outraged. One felt encouraged. One wanted vengeance, but secretly longed for more. Their lives were hopelessly intertwined, meshed now. It was a danse macabre that would ultimately spin out of control. And in a hurry. They could not be happy except in the pursuit of each other. Except Stacey. She wanted to leave everyone and everything behind. She wanted to rely on herself. Just her and her stolen pick-up. She thought as she drove along.

She thought primarily about her mother. Would her mother be able to suffer another shock, another loss? Both her children gone. Stacey wept thinking of her mother after her heart attack. She had been such a vibrant woman always on the go, busy doing something anything, to make a better life for herself and the ones she cared about. And then he had used her heart attack as a further way of controlling her. Illness in a relationship is often exploited. That is one reason Stacey did not show weakness of any kind. Even kindness was often mistaken for weakness, Stacey considered.

Soon she was in Tallahassee, Florida, two and half hours outside and to the west of Jacksonville. Formelli was on the bus headed for his first major stop and layover in Atlanta. Lashonda Williams, after waiting in her office all day and attending to her other duties, biting her nails and watching the clock, went out to Formelli's trailer and found he was gone. He had skipped town it seemed, and he had violated his probation, and that rubbed her the wrong way. This cracker isn't going to get away with this, she thought.

Stacey was a little hungry and a little hung over from the wine. She knew there were fast food restaurants in Tallahassee where she could get a quick bite and then keep plowing west. Formelli's Greyhound made a stop at every podunky little town in Georgia on the way to Atlanta. It ate up considerable time and he was also watching the clock. He had to put up with it. He could not afford to fly and did not have his identification since Stacey had lifted his wallet. He had paid cash for his bus ticket and no one had asked any questions.

Lashonda called her boss and arranged a few days travel time. She was going to bring Formelli back in and have him locked up. She hated white people and she did not even know why. Her parents had hated white people. And their parents had and their parents before them had been slaves. Maybe that was reason enough. Lashonda distrusted whites. They spoke such nice words, but they never meant what they said. She had recently been passed over for a promotion from her supervisor, a white man. The job had gone to another white man with less seniority than she.

Lashonda was not sure where Formelli might have gone, so she had to piece together a route from what she knew of him. She knew he had cop buddies, one or two that still talked to him. She would start there. It was a personal vendetta. She hated Formelli, she hated cops because she could never qualify to be one since she had failed the psyche exam three times in a row. She hated white people, and she hated the fact that this man thought he could skip out on all that. She needed him. She felt a deep desire to abuse him. Furthermore, she knew she would find him. She started looking for an officer named Jim Berea. He was Formelli's close friend still. If anyone knew where Formelli had gone, it would be him.

Stacey got off the road just west of Tallahassee and grabbed a hamburger, fries, and a coke. She went in and ate. She then walked back out to Formelli's truck, the one she had hijacked, and rifled through her things for a toothbrush and toothpaste. She went back inside the fast food joint and brushed her teeth. She also took her make-up off and let her hair down. She was thinking of dying it blonde when she got a hotel room. She figured if she pressed on through and did not have any problems with her vehicle that she could make New Orleans by about seven in the morning. She would spend the day there. A plan was hatching and she wanted to see where it took her.

Lashonda Williams got in touch with Jim Berea. He had no idea where his friend Mario had gone, and was even surprised that he had missed a probation appointment, because to hear Jim tell it, Mario planned to go in front of the judge and have his probation shortened.

"Ain't gonna happen now," Lashonda said. "If you hear from him, call me," Lashonda told the cop and gave him her card. Fucking niggers, Berea thought. "Ain't gonna happen," he mumbled under his breath. When she walked off, he threw the card away. Lashonda went back to the school, where Formelli worked. Maybe someone there had seen something.

Formelli arrived in Atlanta and had to change buses. He had a two hour layover. From Atlanta he would go to New Orleans with a stop at every little cracker town in between. He would make it to New Orleans tomorrow afternoon. Maybe he would get off the bus and rent a car. It would be faster. How to rent a car without any ID was going to be tough. Stacey had even taken Formelli's fake cop badge. It was on his wallet. Maybe there was a cop supply store he could track down in Atlanta. He could buy another fake badge and maybe pass it off as a real one. At least Stacey had not taken his gun.

Three lives, and including Roger Whitaker and his wife, Stacey's mom, five lives now horribly intertwined. The danse had become so twisted, so macabre. They all hated each other. They all needed each other. Only Stacey saw with clear vision. And she had to go. Lashonda searched for Formelli, who searched for Stacey, and her father searched for his daughter. They ached for each other.

Stacey barreled quickly down I-10. She was making good time. She wanted to meet a former lover at Tulane. He had given her the bottoms she wore to dinner with Formelli. She thought wistfully about her little goomba. For once, she thought she might miss a john . She reached down between her legs and parted her panties, glancing down just for a moment. It took only a moment. As Stacey drove along masturbating herself, a truck, a fully loaded semi-tractor trailer, ran across the expressway onto her side. It appeared the driver had a stroke. He hit Stacey head on, and she was decapitated.

She had always had to go. Going had become her life. Now she was gone. Her final thought was of her mom.

#######

The Adventures of Franchesska
by
Cameron H. Chambers

Volume One, Installments 1, 2, and 3
Volume One, Installment One

Franchesska Re-Visits Earth: 2040
by
Cameron H. Chambers

It was around dusk in the bustling city of Savannah, Georgia. The year on earth was 2040, and the once small and stately town of Savannah had grown to a population of almost seven million. Alien species abounded, but they were mostly too clever to be caught by the watchful CIA, which organization routinely imprisoned aliens from other planets and galaxies and tortured and sold them. The ranks of aliens in government were vast, but they mostly fought and feuded over petty details and nothing was ever accomplished. Most, if not all, social services had fallen into disarray. Unemployment was nearly twenty-five percent, worse among certain populations. The food supply had run out, except for the GMOs, genetically modified organisms. These items, like milk, bread, cheese, and meat were cheap and abundant but lacked nutritional value, so, in essence, the more the earthlings ate, the more they starved themselves and their bodies.

Franchesska had not been lost on earth since the French Revolution. That piece of history was characterized by a peasant uprising that overthrew the tyrannical French government. She had spent some time in a prison cell then, and was nervous about landing on earth again though she hoped she would not be there long. And she was hungry. Time travel often had that effect upon her. She climbed the flight of stairs that had opened briefly; it was unnoticed by anyone but her and was from below a bus stop, and she sensed immediately her doom if she did not get off the streets. She turned into a small pizza parlor near the Savannah River in the old part of the city. There she immediately espied Carl, a man she had known for a few months one summer on a visit to the Pleiades.

Carl was drinking beers by himself when he saw Franchesska saunter nearby.

"Can I buy you a beer, Chess?" he asked. Chess was Franchesska's nickname and it suited her.

"Sure. How have you been?" Franchesska said.

"I am miserable. I got married," he answered. Franchesska let out a light hearted giggle. Carl took a closer look at his old friend. Franchesska had smoky grey, almost black, mascara around her upper lids painted up from her brown soulful eyes. She wore a skin tight black latex top that hinted at her 36 DD breasts enough to make any man drool, and she stood five feet ten inches. On this day she wore three inch heels and towered over six feet tall. She weighed about a buck forty, and her long brown hair fell down in luscious loops. Carl had always thought she was Italian or perhaps Bosnian, but Franchesska's papers were American and she spoke excellent, colloquial English. She had always been a bit of an enigma to Carl. She never spoke about where she was from or her childhood. He never knew why she had disappeared from him late one night. Truth be told, Chess had enjoyed Carl's company, but she found the overpopulated and overly polluted Pleiades too much to handle, so when a worm hole had opened, she left. Such is often the case with time travelers. They go out for a pack of cigarettes and never return.

Franchesska was from the Realm, a cluster of many fine stars in the southeast quadrant of the universe. Earth is on the cusp of the southwest and northwest quadrants. The stars of the Realm contain lush jungles and rain forests, mountains of glass and ice, beautiful tropical oceans, a great source of clean fuel and energy and a very happy populace of travelers that are always glad when they are able to go home. But time travel is a tricky proposition at best. One can get stuck on a freeway that goes on for parsec after parsec and not know where he or she is going or landing, until the traveler finally finds an opportunity to get off. And the citizens of the Realm were duty bound to go out of their comfortable confines and try to make the universe a better place until they could settle down, which invariably they once again chose their home planets to do so. Each of them was given a mission to fulfill as well, and the citizen of the Realm never knew he or she had even fulfilled the mission until it was time to come home.

"Let's order a pizza," Chess said. "I am famished."

"You go ahead. I barely have money for another drink. I haven't worked in six months," Carl said.

"I have money. I want a large pizza with all the toppings. And two more beers, please," Franchesska told the waitress. The two got up from the bar and sat at a booth. "So how is she?"

"No, I don't mind. My car is out back. We can be there in ten minutes."

"Perfect," Chess said. Well played, she thought to herself. She had gotten a meal, met a friend, and was about to have a place to sleep. She guessed another worm hole would open in the morning, and she could leave earth, hopefully for good.

The pair arrived safely back at Carl's apartment. "Nice apartment," Franchesska commented. It was sarcastic but not meant to do injury.

"I know. Remember my old place. We could shut out the world. Here I am on a busy thoroughfare and can't sleep half the time."

"I remember. Draw the blinds," Chess said. "How about some tea?"

"I've got that. Zen, your favorite. I still drink it."

"Marvelous," Chess said while Carl heated the water.

"This stove is 110, so do you want to take a shower first? The water will take a while to boil. I could use a shower too."

"Sure. I always like it when someone soaps my back," Chess said. They undressed in the dimly lit bathroom and got in the shower. The water was lukewarm and the pressure was poor. Chess soaped up, as did Carl, and they sprayed each other with the massager. Then a bell went off in the apartment. "What is that?" Chess asked alarmed. She thought the CIA was at the door.

"There's thirty seconds of water left. Let me get the shampoo out of your hair." Chess had forgotten that during one presidential administration all showers were cut down to three minutes and water regulators were placed in every home. They climbed out of the shower. Chess leaned over the sink, her butt sticking out seductively, and Carl did not need another hint. He grabbed her ass and she spun around and kissed him. He moved his hands up to her ample breasts, and then he sucked on her generous tits. She began to moan. She turned back around and bent over the sink and spread her long legs. Carl was erect. Pleaidean men usually have large members, but it was not that which Chess enjoyed so much about Carl, but rather the way he worked it. He thrust deep inside her and pulled almost entirely out and thrust deep again repeatedly. His rhythm was slow at first and then gathered speed till they both came and let out a hearty laugh of carnal pleasure in unison. The tea kettle in the adjoining small kitchen screamed its approval.

"Oh, thank you, sweetheart. I needed that. It seems I have been traveling forever," Chess said.

"Yes, that was nice. Let's have some tea."

They drank their tea and then Carl folded the bed out from the wall. They rested, but Chess did not sleep. She checked her cell phone. There was the same worm hole opening up in about forty-five minutes. She could walk there if she left now. As she got up from bed, Carl stirred and asked where she was going. "Nowhere" she answered, but she knew he understood her to be lying.

"You got away once. Take me with you. I have nothing here."

"You don't understand. I am not like you, Carl. I am not merely an alien."

"What are you then, and keep your voice down, the CIA has bugs everywhere."

"I am a time traveler, and I am trying to get back home. I have never told anyone this."

"They exist?"

"Yes. I have said too much. I must go."

"I am coming."

"Okay, but don't be afraid."

Carl and Chess drove to the bus stop where she had seen

the flight of stairs. She could tell the worm hole was getting ready to open. Carl could not see anything unusual. Then it opened. Carl was shocked to see the flight of stairs descending into nothingness that had not been there before. "Come on. We only have a few seconds." They went to the bottom of the stairs, and Franchesska's cell phone flashed the following message, "Welcome home...you are now returning to the Realm." She was overjoyed. She had completed her mission.

Volume One, Installment Two

Franchesska and Carl on the Realm
by,
Cameron H. Chambers

The beams of colorful light streaked by Franchesska and Carl with maddening alacrity.

"What is happening?" Carl cried out. He felt very sick to his stomach. He regurgitated.

Franchesska laughed. "It happens the first few times you time travel. It will be over soon." She grasped his hand to steady him. Then they could see the Realm coming into view, and they were gently touching down on the planet's surface. Franchesska was home. It had been a few decades as measured in earth time, which is a concept that really has no meaning to a time traveler, since she had been home. Franchesska was a member of a race of Immortals. She would shed her body in the usual lifetime for an Immortal from her planet and then be given a new one. A body was a concept that did not really fit with Franchesska's race of Immortals either. It was more like a pulsating shell.

"What is this place?" Carl asked.

"It is my home. The Realm. You are safe here and you may stay here as long as you like. Or my family will arrange transport to another planet for you if you like. Or you can stay with me. My mother is the Queen. My father is the King."

"That makes you a princess," Carl said.

Franchesska laughed. "Yes, this will all be mine some day. But seeing as how my parents are Immortals, it could be a while. They have to step down first. Would you care to look around with me? It has been a very long time since I have been home."

"Where are your parents?"

"Oh, they will be around to summon me. They know we are here. Would you like to get some more pizza? I am famished," Franchesska said.

"Maybe some soup. That was kind of a rough ride," Carl said. Franchesska pointed and he turned around, and they saw an eatery called "Joe's Soup and Pizza Emporium."

"Okay, here's a place," Franchesska said. They went inside. It was a facsimile of a fifties diner from earth. It was resplendent with red suede booths and a long counter with black leather stools trimmed in chrome. There was a juke box playing Elvis and a terrific malt dispenser. The tables were a brown melamine, and on the walls were posters of suped-up hot rods. They were seated, and Carl ordered a large bowl of chicken and noodle soup and a coke, and Franchesska ordered a pizza with the works and a beer.

"What currency do they take here?" Carl asked.

"Oh, you don't have to pay for anything here. All goods and services are free on the Realm," Franchesska said. "We have evolved past money. We are creatures for lack of a better word of energy. We can shape or pattern anything merely from our minds or the minds of others. Our minds give off enough energy to turn anything you see here into reality. You have to note that I am not in my true form. We simply keep shape and form for visitors. Our visitors have to eat and sleep and receive medical treatment occasionally. We provide all that though none of our people needs it," Franchesska said.

"So then what are you?" Carl asked.

"We are pure energy. This is not my natural form, but I adopted it when I met you, and somehow I got stuck in this form, but I am home now. I am no longer traveling. I had to trust you with my secret, and in so doing I completed my mission. You are a great treasure to me, my dear." Franchesska leaned in over Carl's bowl of homemade chicken soup and kissed him. She wiped the chicken broth off her lips.

"That is quite good," she said, referring to the chicken soup. "Eat up." Franchesska took a swig of her beer. "Would you like a massage, or would you like to see my penthouse?"

"The penthouse, I think," Carl said.

The waiter brought Franchesska a key to the outer door. He said everything was the way she had left it in her penthouse. She thanked the waiter and asked how things had been on the planet.

"Everything has been fine with the Realm, but we have missed you. You were gone so long," the waiter said.

Franchesska thanked the waiter again. "Let's go to my little place. I am sure you will like it," she said to Carl. "You can rest."

"Let's go," he said. "I think that was the best chicken and noodle soup I have ever had. It tasted just like my mother's recipe."

Franchesska laughed.

They caught a taxi to One Realm Place. The taxi was black and white with fuzzy dice hanging from the rear view mirror, and inside the cab played soulful Latin music. It might have been Selena. One Realm Place was a high rise with about sixty floors, it appeared to Carl. It was a doorman building. Franchesska owned the penthouse, she had said, and she had a private elevator. She said a hearty greeting to the doorman. She called him by name. She didn't really own the penthouse. There was no ownership on the Realm. Things merely were so, this way and that, in an ever changing landscape. She simply informed Carl she owned the penthouse to put him at ease.

The penthouse was two bedrooms, trimmed in white, and had fabulous paintings that appeared to be originals on the walls, with an adjoining living room, also white and one red brick wall, and a good sized eat-in kitchen, a spectacular bath done in black onyx, and a terrace with a garden, growing lush red and green fruits. There were different views of the Realm from each window of the penthouse. Carl noticed a misty mountain that resembled Mt. Fuji from Franchesska's bedroom. He saw the Eiffel Tower from her living room. There was a huge jungle on the other side of the penthouse contained within what looked like Central Park in New York. And from the bathroom was a fabulous Ice palace. It was more of an ice castle set up on a cloud covered hill. Carl walked back into the living room. Franchesska said, "watch this." She looked at the fireplace, which was an authentic wood burning fireplace, and it ignited. Carl noted it gave off heat.

"How did you do that?" Carl asked.

"I can do many, many things," Franchesska said with a lighthearted giggle. "Would you like a brandy?"

"Sure," Carl said. He could not believe his luck at having hitched his wagon to Franchesska's star once again. Now that she was done traveling, maybe things could last between them. He was never returning to earth, as Franchesska had said she wasn't either. And Carl's wife could keep his disability payments since there would be no divorce. She would be happier with that than with Carl. She was all about the money and nothing else. He did not miss her.

"One second," Franchesska said. She walked into the bath, and soon emerged in a slinky little number meant to excite Carl's every desire. She walked out into the living room with sheer black stockings on that ran to the top of her girlish thighs, and a black thong, delicious and inviting, and she was topless. Her 36 DD tits had glitter on them and were magnificent, perky and firm. She wore three inch black high heels. She called out loud, "play the music of the gods." The most beautiful and seductive music played in the living room. She walked across the room toward Carl, who was lounging on the sofa sipping his brandy, and grabbed him by the shirt collar. He carefully put down his drink and followed cue and stood up.

Franchesska took his shirt off over his head and zipped down his pants and took off his shoes. She bent down in a crouching position and took his member into her mouth. She sucked it. She bit softly around his penis, and sucked his balls. Carl moaned appreciatively. She went up and down on his member with her right hand, all the while sucking it, and eventually Carl came in great pleasure. He cried out. It was wonderful. He was exhausted and spent. Franchesska pushed him down on the sofa, and put a blanket over him. She turned off the overhead light and went out on the terrace. Carl fell asleep immediately. He slept so solidly and the air was so good, he did not even snore.

Franchesska turned into a small, glowing ball of light. She was smaller than a beach ball, but larger than a basketball. She pulsated with an orange and green light that went within and outside of her, as she hovered over her terrace about four feet off the ground.

"Welcome back, dear," her mother said.

"Yes, it has been some time," her father said.

"I missed you so much," Franchesska said.

"It is over now," her mother said. "You are free once again."

"Chess, you may go anywhere and do anything," her father said.

"Thank you so much. I love you both," Franchesska said. Just then she jumped from the terrace and transformed back into the creature she had assumed for Carl. Her brown locks were caught in the wind, flowing majestically behind her. She was followed by a rich stream of thousands of Monarch butterflies as she gently touched down on the street below. She thought she would do some grocery shopping for Carl. Of course, she didn't have to do this, but she really felt like leaving her apartment. He would sleep for awhile, and she would prepare the both of them a large dinner. She felt good inside. It was nice to be home and have a companion.

Volume One, Installment Three

Franchesska Hits the Mean Streets
by,
Cameron H. Chambers

Franchesska was finally back home and on the streets of her hometown, a lovely contemporary village on the Realm. The first thing she did, as she was walking along, was turn herself invisible. One would think this would preclude anyone from seeing Chess. But all Chess' compatriots and fellow residents of the Realm were able to see her, as were visiting higher order aliens who had the ability to see invisibility. It is not so hard to see invisibility if you know what you are looking for. Right there on the street, Chess stripped off her clothes. She had worn them, with a change of outfit or two, for a couple of decades while time traveling, and while still perfectly fresh and clean, she felt constrained by them. In general, she did not like wearing clothes, even though she could create a very fashionable wardrobe at will. She remained in her magnificent body with the delicious 36 DD breasts, the body she time traveled in. Her round, firm ass bobbed up and down as she walked on the wide, generous sidewalks, and her girlish hips swayed rhythmically. She could hear music playing. It was pleasant and comforting. She loved being home. She was first greeted by the Royal Guard. Bot One asked her if she was fine in a very polite manner. Bot One said, "How is my liege? We have missed you. "

"Fine Bot One. How have things been?"

"Everything is under control, my liege," Bot One answered.

"Carry on. Good to see you, Bot Two," Chess answered.

"Thank you, my liege." Bot Two never spoke unless spoken to.

The Royal Guard is comprised of over one hundred thousand robots and special functioning Androids, all at Franchesska's command. They were a gift from her parents. The Royal Guard was primarily tasked with defending the planet, not that there had been an invasion attempt in eons. Only Bot One and Bot Two were allowed to speak directly to Chess. The remaining numbers merely carried out commands. The Bots could see invisibility and turn invisible as Bot One or Bot Two or their generals commanded. And back in their days as warriors, there can be no mistake. They were ruthless. They maintained all the higher order functioning skills of the members of the Realm, but were not pure energy. They were creations, created by Chess' father a long time ago when he went to war. And they could assume any form, but they generally liked to appear as holograms or holographic images and very often as flying creatures, akin to birds. They were indestructible in this way.

So Chess meandered on foot out of town. It could be a very short walk or a long walk, as she chose. She came to a grand waterfall over five hundred feet high in the air and went in for a swim. The blue water cascaded down around her, juxtaposed with the brown boulders that lay in the water and on the white, sandy shore. The lush forest encircling the waterfall had grown up for centuries, and there were a multitude of colorful flowers along the shoreline, some green, some a brilliant orange, some a fiery red, and some a deep blue. Many of the flowers were creations. Chess' mom had the green thumb. She loved to garden and create species of flowers and placed them throughout the largish planet and its sister stars. She had been at it for quite some time, so the Realm was very lush with every landscape imaginable.

There were deserts, and dozens of moons, multiple suns, lush tropical rain forests, grand oceans, cities of glass, towering mountains, placid lakes, white water rivers, all more beautiful and breath taking when viewed than the previous scene. Chess tarried in the waterfall a time. The water was perfect. Back in Franchesska's penthouse, Carl woke up from his dream-imaged sleep and felt refreshed and vibrant. He could not remember sleeping so well. There had always been something that kept him wide awake. He had to use the bathroom, but he did not know where it was. He stood by the side of the bed, a grand, over-sized four poster, richly carved and engraved Victorian with modern and comfortable mattresses, and looked for a door. He said out loud, "bathroom door open." A door appeared and popped open.

He could see inside that there were the usual amenities for a bathroom: a sink, a toilet, a shower. "Is it safe to enter?" he asked.

A voice said, "yes." He did not recognize the voice. Carl did not envy the idea of being stuck in a bathroom, traveling through space and time, and always having to find an appropriate men's room to push on to the next dimension. He did not understand time travel. He barely believed Chess could do it. It seemed somehow undignified to be trapped in a lavatory for the ages, and he did not want to leave Chess, and he was getting more than a little nervous, finding she was not in bed with him. He entered the bathroom and sat down on the toilet. When it was time to flush, he saw a chain hanging from the ceiling that he had not noticed before. He was starting to like the Realm very much. There was no type of invention anymore on the Pleaides. It had become stagnant. A cesspool. That is why such great numbers had migrated to earth. It had become all about survival there, and though Chess had found him on earth, he secretly feared he would have to make a getaway back to his home planet one day. He shuddered at the thought. He pulled the chain, and the toilet flushed, making a rather voluminous sound, but down came crystal clear and clean, nearly freezing water in a gallon or two from the ceiling dumped right on his head. He heard Chess giggle.

"That was not nice," Carl said. Chess giggled again.

"Time to wake up," she said. Carl could hear her voice audibly even though she was not present in her apartment. This had him worried.

"Can you hear and see whatever I do?" Or am I going crazy?" he said.

"No, mon ami, you are not crazy," Chess said.

"This puts me at a distinct disadvantage."

"Men are always at a disadvantage. You will get used to it," Chess said.

"Where are you?"

"Turn on the television," Chess said.

Carl walked into the living room and said, " television on." Nothing happened. He said it three more times in a variety of commands. Still nothing happened. Chess giggled again though more wholeheartedly this time.

"Try the remote and you will see me," Chess said. "You mortals are so much fun," Chess said sincerely. She could have turned the television on at his first command, but she liked playing a game or two with her partner. Her lover would learn to appreciate this about her. They were always fun affairs.

Carl flicked on the remote and on screen was two elephants mating. Chess giggled. "Change the channel," she said.

"What channel is it?" Carl asked.

"Pick one." He did so and saw Chess naked, who had changed from her cloak of invisibility, with her long brown hair, wet and draped around her stylish shoulders and her perfectly trimmed bush, looking very sultry and beckoning.

"I like this channel," Carl said. "But I am starving."

"Go to the fridge."

He opened the refrigerator in the smallish kitchen just off the living room, and there he found Gouda cheese, seedless red grapes, lunch meat, and many more items, all his favorites. "I might get used to this," he said.

"You will, and you will learn many things from me, and we will be very happy till you pass."

I am going to die?"

"You are mortal, Carl. One day you will die. But we have many extraordinary memories to make first."

"What happens when I die?"

"There are only certain things I can tell you, but I can tell you that you will be reborn. I am not allowed to be more specific than that. It would not do you any good if I was," Franchesska said.

"How long do we have together?" he said.

"The proper amount of time. I cannot be more specific than that. I will give you a hint and tell you that you live to a ripe old age and in good health till it is your time. I am immortal. I have always been, and I will always be. Now turn around."

Carl spun around, and Chess planted a kiss on his lips. She was in the kitchen beside him. She turned his shoulders first toward the bedroom and then slapped him on the ass playfully. They went into the bedroom.

#######

Technologic Advances in the "Baby Boom" and "X" and "Y" Generations and Introducing "GenZyme"

This was originally written as a blog in the year 2009 A.D.

It is somewhat widely accepted that the youngest of the Baby Boomers was born in 1966. This puts me among the youngest of the Boomers as I was born in the early 60s. The oldest Boomers are considered to have been born immediately following World War II, so a considerable block of them are now in their sixties and soon in their seventies. This in turn makes the youngest, not the oldest, of the subsequent generation, generation X, known also as Gen X, born in 1986 or thereabouts; however, some would say the youngest of Gen X was born as early as 1980. The oldest Gen Xers were born somewhere around 1966 after the Boomers. These individuals, Gen Xers born in the late 60s, at present would be in their early to mid-forties or fifties. Many of the oldest of Gen Y, also born some time just after 1986 or so, who are sometimes referred to as Gen Why or the MTV Generation, attend our institutions of higher learning now, and many of the younger members of this generation currently fall into the categories that comprise our tweens and teenagers.

This means ZGen or GenZyme has begun to make its way into the world in the last year or so. Of course, these dates are somewhat relative and are actually non-specific, as a generation is not an exact number of years. Many of my friends are Gen X and an expected addition to a friend's family, the mother being a Gen Y, should eventually—her child—be one of the older members of GenZyme. Now, more commonly referred to as millennials. It is not unusual to have four generations in the same family on the planet at the same time, and sometimes a fifth, which would represent a span of one hundred years or so, maybe more, maybe less, depending on years of birth.

Technology is a very interesting study and can as much define its generation as its wars, assassinations, music, haircuts, dress, movies, cars, and television programs. I don't remember the Golden Era of Hollywood firsthand; I believe it took place in the 1950s, so I was not yet alive, but I more or less remember the 60s and thereafter. I was present for much of the Cold War, which began in the 50s, and I was around when the Berlin Wall came down. And I have lived to witness the Cold War heat up all over again. Every generation has its moments, and these moments in time are often shared across the lines of various generations.

I have seen a number of advancements in automobiles, airplanes, and boats to name just a few handy items, before the onset of the Ys in the mid 1980s and the advent of very labor intensive computers and subsequently the popularity of the Internet, and I clearly remember a day when getting somewhere by means of one of these conveyances was not a huge pain in the derriere like it is today. Transport may, however, face another revolution during my lifetime. This uprising I would say is likely, but it may not be what you expect.

I have heard various bits of information, but as yet have not looked seriously into the matter, that some clever inventor has developed a working prototype of a teleportation device. I understand right now it can be used only for inanimate objects. I think there was a successful trial involving an orange. This innovation could, hopefully at least, transform shipping as we now know it. Imagine actually having your bags waiting for you at the hotel by the time you get there, and not carelessly winging their way to parts unknown, as happens about fifty percent of the time at present. Or imagine having no need to lug heavy, cumbersome belongings through airport after airport. But then this working prototype of a teleportation device may well be a hoax. But if it is, it is probable it won't remain a hoax forever.

Given the premise that technology tends to advance at an exponential rate, not a linear one, then what I see ahead for the remainder of my life could be truly amazing or things could just turn into a much worse pile of dung. But that is always the possibility. C'est la vie. Gen Yers are the truly mobile members of our heretofore brief crawl across the global landscape as a species. They have diverse communication devices and cell phones with every type of convenience: Internet, email, cell phones, GPS, music and video downloads for a quick getaway. There are maps and driving routes, to include voice-automated command and visual displays, and everything imaginable for the most highly tech-oriented and mobile generation so far.

I find a touch of irony in their flight to mobility. I see this as a trend that will reverse itself. Gen Yers will likely become much less mobile and more sedentary because of the development of virtual reality, which, as a prototype, has stemmed from the minds of baby boomers.

Perhaps the preceding generation or two play out little dramas or nasty tricks on the ones to follow and involve the next generation or several subsequent ones completely in their ill-advised activities, often without fair warning. This I would suggest is a similar model to generational selling on some level, or locking in product sales over the various generations to follow. The baby boomers did one thing fantastically: market products and services. The next generations become so inundated by notions of what they think they need or want, that there is little or no sales resistance left to muster or consider.

The virtual world will most likely show significant improvements made by Generation Xers and Yers, and could have much greater impact than its somewhat limited one now, some sources predict by as early as 2014. For those investors out there, you might be advised to buy the stocks of virtual companies; not companies that are virtual, but rather companies that enhance the reality of virtual reality. These goods and services, which will likely become their own industry soon, could catch on huge. So in the near future, there may be much less of a need for most of us to go anywhere in physical space and time, owing to the new frontier of virtual reality products. For those without a proper working definition, Science.org states "virtual reality is an artificial environment created by computers, in which people can immerse themselves and feel that this artificial reality really does exist."

And every day along come more and more members of GenZyme. Let the generational sales issue forth upon the unsuspecting. If global population trends, which also expand exponentially, and not in a linear fashion, continue, then it is likely that in the day of most GenZymes, or millennials, if you prefer, it really will be almost impossible for anyone to go anywhere. So, we will all sit at home and virtualize. It could be a recluse's nightmare or dream, depending on how one looks at it, and I guess what his or her experience is with the virtual product line. Owing to what the population is soon likely to be, we might have to wait in long lines for trams to convey us down the grocery aisles of huge warehouses where we are completely unable to find what we are looking for. You think Wal-Mart and Sam's are big right now. Just wait. That is, of course, provided there is no scarcity of food. Resources, including water, will become very limited.

In the case of teleportation being perfected, and assuming we can't send along living creatures by this method for quite some time, if at all, perhaps due to incompatible and complex DNA structures, then shipping your luggage or a jar of pickles may be one of its more practical uses. And that could mean for the GenZyme populous and many of us lingering on the planet that our bags might have much greater frequency of arriving at the proper destination in a timely fashion, than we do. But then it is possible we will never leave home again. It might be time to think about securing credit for that swimming pool you have always wanted, or putting in a hot tub, or perhaps at least, putting up that privacy fence. We would no longer be able to effectively travel in real space, and it would be debatable if we would even feel the desire or need, but our attaché could still chalk up all the frequent flyer miles it wanted. Hmm...objects transported willy-nilly through space to any destination. I wonder what this means for the war on terror.

Virtual reality has me a little confused and raises some puzzling questions. I'm not very familiar with it on a practical basis, only a little bit on a conceptual one. Feeling something is real and it actually being real is kind of a dicey proposition. It is probably best left to semanticists, doctors, scientists, and video game makers to define reality nowadays. My first question is: how real is the feeling of something being real going to feel? And will we have an enhanced understanding of reality through virtual reality or will it just seem real but in actuality be more like a really lousy reality show? And how real is real anyway? And how real do we want real to be?

These newest technologies also beg the question: will it be possible for an individual to teleport a real item or real object into virtual reality? Let's assume I am in a virtual world traversing The Great Wall of China or climbing Mount Everest, and I remember that I need something that I didn't bring along to my latest of programmed realities. It could be a backpack, a sandwich, an oxygen tent, a Sherpa, whatever. I am about to defeat Mount Everest. I don't want to quit my computer-enhanced conquest. Is it possible that the absent item, whatever it is, could be teleported into my virtual reality, and since it would be a concrete article, (let's not include Sherpas in this; since they are sentient beings, their DNA is probably incompatible at present) will this gadget or device work properly in a virtual setting? Perhaps I should just get up and get the item myself, say if it happens to be a sandwich or a compass or such. There most likely will be a pause button.

Will there be such a thing as virtual hunger pains, and if so, could eating a virtual hamburger quench them? Could McDonalds at some point have served ten billion virtual customers? And is virtual reality addictive? Many individuals say video games are, and I have seen what Internet chat can do to a household. Might there be in the future virtual reality interventions? And I have another all imposing question, as I mentioned above. Will I be able to, or want to, or know to, pause virtual reality, so I can get up and walk around if my foot falls asleep? This prospect of putting reality on hold, might give a virtual world a distinct advantage over "real" reality. But isn't reality just really reality at any rate? I don't know. Maybe not.

Notions like these are for much greater minds than mine to consider. I am relatively certain of one statement, however. Cogito ergo sum. It is Latin for "I think, therefore I am." So by extrapolation, I exist, therefore I am real. By virtue of the fact that I am real, does that mean I exist in virtual reality? Things might not seem real at all in the not so distant future, or reality may be entirely too much with us. As Einstein once said, "reality is merely an illusion, albeit a persistent one." At least, I think Einstein was real. And I think these were really his words and they were real too. Or maybe what we all see and hear is virtual already, a la "The Matrix," and the timer hasn't popped off on our programmed adventure. I wonder if there is anyone left that can teleport me out of here. Maybe not. Am I already imprisoned in a holodeck? Is this all some sort of image, like a hologram? There are scientists who believe the entire universe is merely an image. So are any of us real, and is any of this real, and, if this is just one big hologram, where is the true reality? I think I'll just get up and fix a sandwich instead of worrying about it. Now where is that jar of pickles? Will you please teleport to me a jar of Kosher dills? Addictions and cravings might be the only real part of us.

Random Stories from the Streets (a serialized article)
by
Cameron H. Chambers

Being a down and out artist is not a new story. In fact, this is just a twist on a story that dates back to the earliest reaches of civilization. Orwell was there when he wrote Down and Out in Paris and London. Also, when he worked for the British Empire in Burma, he was a significant outsider looking in. I am not comparing myself to George Orwell. He is a far better writer and essayist than I shall ever be. I do know the bitterly mean streets and alleyways of my city, however. I have now spent a good bit of time on the streets though I am not officially homeless. It is another world, an underbelly, and not of necessity always unseemly or grotesque.

I come by my fate naturally enough. I am a life-long sufferer of mental illness, since my earliest recollections around age fourteen or fifteen. I am now in my late fifties. Not just one mental illness, either, I was doubly blessed. Whoever stated a burden is never too much. I attempted suicide twice during previous episodes. I lay in a coma for two nights after one attempt. My last battle with schizophrenia and bi-polar disorder, I lost my health, of course, my livelihood, my car, my house, my freedom, and every possession I had known, not to mention two of my very best friends, and a third very promising friendship. The monsters of bad brain circuitry and errant chemicals had conspired again. It was a harsh judgment to go to prison this time, when, in essence, I had done absolutely nothing wrong, and was fleeing a city I had envisioned as Hell, and was quite afraid to be buried there. Again.

This is the briefest of stories of what entailed after I reasserted my right to continue.

Random Stories from the Streets (a serialized article)
by
Cameron H. Chambers

Three years ago I had a stroke. I lost everything. I have rebuilt my life nicely. It is simply a process. I have done it now about five times from scratch. But during my problems with epilepsy, a stroke, and high blood pressure, my bi-polar type two disorder kicked in again. It was very disheartening. A well-intentioned family member thought that commitment of me was in order. He swore that he was trying to help. Commitment is probably the worst thing that can ever happen to anyone. It is a prison sentence with very low functioning and typically ill individuals, some of whom are quite dangerous and without proper judgment due to their maladies. The paperwork for the commitment was not even legal, or questionable at best.

The hospital where I was stuffed and kept away was later brought up on federal racketeering charges and false imprisonment charges, as well as Medicare and Medicaid fraud investigations, or so I heard that second part, but I have no idea of the outcomes of the cases. My thought, and it has persisted, is that several dirty cops were getting kick backs for placing individuals into this institution under the Baker Act, whether it was warranted or not. The hospital paid them in cash. The hospital then in turn soaked the patients for their insurance and refused to release them in a timely manner, according to the law of the Baker Act in the State of Florida, which allows for mandatory holding time of up to 72 hours only, but only if the patient is a threat to himself or others. As part of a fake or bogus or non-binding legal commitment proceeding, I was under an Ex Parte Motion, which allows my forced observation of up to one week, provided I am treated within 24 hours of arriving at the facility. I was kept almost four months.

So this led to a near foreclosure of my house, the loss of several months of disability payments, and confinement that I allege was unlawful. I, as well, lost thousands in equity when I was finally able to have my house sold. I was even attacked twice in this hospital. And one of the times was by staff, a group of seven or eight men. Another time it was an individual, who I believe was using the hospital as an escape from incarceration and was actually arrested for felony charges. There is a nasty series of events quite often that the mentally ill must deal with in their own lives, aside from being persecuted and prosecuted. So for a time, I was more or less on the streets, but really just afraid to go home.

I will have my closure soon enough, and as for those reading this article, I apologize, but let this go as fair warning to what a cesspool it has become out there. Human instinct is now ruled by two of its more basic equations: the need for sex, cheap, tawdry or otherwise, and the need to purchase objects, both of which unfortunately go hand-in-hand quite often.

#######